NIGHT SHIFT

Written and illustrated by

HENRY BREWIS

FARMING PRESS

First published 1996

A catalogue record for this book is available from the British Library
ISBN 0 85236 364 8

**Published by Farming Press
Miller Freeman Professional Ltd
Wharfedale Road, Ipswich IP1 4LG, United Kingdom**

*Distributed in North America
by Diamond Farm Enterprises,
Box 537, Alexandria Bay, NY 13607, USA*

Typeset by Galleon Typesetting, Ipswich
Printed and bound in Finland by WSOY

NIGHT SHIFT

FOREWORD

Giles is clever and rich. He's on the Euro gravy train, with his snout in the trough and fingers in the till. It's maybe too good to last. . . .

Miss Angela is 'county' and lives in a stately home with her dogs. She's past her best – but a lot tougher than she looks. . . .

Geordie's on the pension, but still shepherding. It's lambing time – two pairs, a hanged single and a yow who smothered a triplet already – but the night has just begun. . . .

Lucy is an 'artist', though not everyone is entirely convinced of this. . . .

Sol is a 'bouncer' at Joanna's on the Quayside. He's built like a byre, wears a ring in his left ear and dark glasses at night. He's not an intellectual.

Trevor lives with three expensive women, overwhelmed by gee-gees, jodhpurs and Bon Jovi. It's not easy, especially when he's trying to balance other people's books. . . .

Kevin fixes things – washing machines, videos, cars that won't start. Once he gets them going, he steals them. He's very good at it. . . .

Gloria has a mysterious visitor – but then she often does. . . .

Wally watched his father sail down the Tyne on a foreign ship years ago, and never saw him again. His mother was delighted. . . .

Foxie can't sleep. Sep's bird scarer is firing outside his

window. He may sue in the morning . . . but in the morning it gets worse. . . .

Shelagh has had enough of the bloody countryside . . . the bleating sheep, the farm traffic, the awful smells. She'd rather be in Birmingham. . . .

Gazza is a leader of 'layabouts' on the Primrose estate, but he has a master plan to make them all rich and famous. . . .

It's a casserole of characters in the same pot.

Politicians may blather about the 'one nation state'. It's a good sound byte, but of course it's a load of rubbish.

The gulf between the new-age traveller squatting in a lay-by, and the chairman of 'Amalgamated Electric' counting his bonus and share options is obvious enough . . . and every city has its enclaves of complacent prosperity and DSS despair . . . as well as a few other conditions in between.

And the countryside, once a simple feudal stew of gentry and peasant, now has several new ingredients. . . .

. . . the out of town townie (who can blame him?)

. . . the eager environmentalist (who can ignore him?)

. . . the righteous rambler (who can stop him?)

. . . the intrusive bureaucrat (who needs him?)

. . . and the thief (who can catch him?)

This little story is primarily about people in the country. Some of them have been there forever, others just a year or two. Some fit easily enough – some don't. Others only come for a stroll . . . and get lost.

CHAPTER ONE

Monday March 25th – according to Mr McCaskill, it was definitely spring . . . but apparently no one had pointed this out to Mother Nature. Maybe she was blooming in Middlesex or Dorset or Devon, but up north the lady was still in dour December mood. Obviously huffed about something. Were those little patches of snow behind the dyke waiting for some more . . . God, he hoped not.

Geordie Dodds at the Glebe Farm reckoned it was one of the worst lambing days he could remember – but to be fair, he said that at least once every year. 'Alright, maybe hardly as bad as Easter '58. . . . Now *that* was a real corker. If you weren't lambin' that weekend, y' knew nowt about bad weather. Terrible day, Good Friday . . . lost thirty lambs that happy holiday – and come t' think of it, '63 wasn't much better. Of course the sheep were all outside then, not like now. These days everything's born under cover –

special pens, clean straw, luxury apartments. Mind you, the sods could still die easily enough . . . well y' know what sheep are like – bloody awkward creatures at the best o' times. . . .'

Geordie's maternity hospital was in the big corrugated iron hayshed, recently extended with a lean-to over the alleyway to the redundant stone byres that stood alongside. It worked well enough. By the end of March most of the hay had been eaten, and at least four bays stood empty. Enough space for 120 lambing ewes, with a run-out into the sheltered stackyard. What's more those old byres and loose boxes provided a very useful line of emergency wards for any difficult cases that might need special attention.

But then, as Geordie said, 'The sheep *have* to go out sometime,' and he would usually give the lambs no more than a couple of days to get 'footy' and full, before he kicked them into the field to take their chances. Well, there just wasn't room for everything. Half a dozen twins, a single, and a set o' triplets born last night. And in any case, the lambs were more likely to pick up some disease if kept too long in those old buildings. And naturally it would be terminal . . . it usually was with sheep.

However, even Geordie's best laid plans 'gang aft a-gley', and on this miserable wet Monday he'd been obliged to 'rescue' a three and a pair, all a week old – and fetch them back inside. One of the triplets was nearly a 'goner', but maybe that wouldn't be a *total* disaster. The yow hadn't enough milk for three anyway. But the twins were empty as well . . . abandoned by a mother more interested in her own greedy belly. She'd just wandered off and left the wee things to fend for themselves. Geordie found them 'sheltering' in the ditch, under the hawthorn hedge, knee deep in water . . . their occasional pathetic bleats quickly blown away on the wind. The yow, apparently unconcerned, stuffing her face miles away.

And she wasn't all that keen to follow him in either. It proved a delicate operation. There he was, looking like a homeless refugee, the rain running down the back of his neck, cap dripping, nose dripping, all-over damp, bent double like a half-closed pocket knife . . . making silly sheep noises, as he slowly dragged the two limp bodies homewards in front of the reluctant mother. He was tempting her to follow, praying she'd stay with him all the way to the dry byre. Perhaps he should have carried some feed with him, a few protein nuts in a sack might've encouraged the greedy bitch to tag along with more enthusiasm . . . But of course all the others would've come galloping over the hill as well, and probably trampled him to death for the last nut.

With a struggle, he got as far as the gate leading into the stackyard, and gently laid the lambs down at mother's nose. They bleated and struggled to their feet, as the yow fussed and gurgled the familiar maternal sounds. Carefully he opened the gate, no sudden movements to shatter this finely balanced manoeuvre. The yow could bolt off at any moment. Geordie could tell she was definitely thinking about it. If he could just get close enough he might make a grab for her, catch her, and drag her under cover before she had any other ideas. (He could come back for the lambs – they certainly wouldn't run far.) He'd have to be absolutely sure though . . . no good making a blind dive, and missing, or just ending up with a handful of wool. That would be hopeless. He knew he had to be more sneaky these days. Gone the time when he could perform a flying tackle on some supersonic gimmer, and roll her into touch like an All-Black wing forward. Aye, maybe once, a long time ago, he could do that . . . shuffle the ewe up agin the hedge, feint to go one way, and get 'er as she bought the dummy. But he

3

was much faster, fitter, younger then . . . his knees didn't creak, his back never complained. . . . He was indestructible, or at least he thought so. . . . That's what he told everybody.

Geordie quietly unhooked the chain, lifting the gate open (not many of Geordie's gates were 'swingers') . . . all the time looking over his shoulder at the fidgety yow. She was still there, sniffing at her half-perished family, stamping her foot, looking agitated. So far so good. Geordie tiptoed back to the lambs, crouching low, bleating his best impersonation of a distressed sheep. God, what a ridiculous way to make a living! His left foot was squelching noisily inside the welly, his big hands wet and freezing cold now, his nose bunged up with snivelly snotty stuff. He sniffed and snorted and spat it out, edging back towards the twins. The yow was right there, head down, the view from her left eye just temporarily obscured by one of the lambs. It was now or never!

Perhaps Geordie's lunge just lacked a little bit of confidence, not quite as positive as years gone by. . . . Simply not quick enough. Whatever it was, the yow must've seen him coming . . . just a glimpse of the right hand darting up to take her round the neck. She spun round. Geordie made a desperate dive for a back leg, and hung on as if his very life depended on this arrest. He was on the ground now, the yow kicking frantically to be free . . . hauling Geordie through the clarts, back towards the open field. He knew if he let go it could take the rest of the day to catch the bastard again . . . might even have to get the whole flock into the yard. And what a performance that would be! There was no way this animal could be allowed to escape. Desperately he managed to claw his left hand up along her flank, and twist her over onto her side, down into the mire beside him. He struggled his way up her body until he had all his weight

4

over the beast, and a hand on her throat, and finally – finally – she surrendered.

That's how his missus found them. The two lambs were still standing shivering by the open gate, and Geordie sitting on top of the yow punching her repeatedly in the face . . . spitting and swearing.

'Are y' alright?' she asked. Doreen was always worried about his heart at lambing time. He got far too excited. The sheep seemed to drive him a bit crazy.

'Champion,' he spluttered. 'We're havin' a grand time, aren't we pet?' He thumped the yow one more time, just for luck, hoisted her onto her feet . . . and with the bewildered beast between his legs, and a firm hold under her chin, 'rode' her into the byre like some kind of clarty cowboy. Doreen followed with the lambs. She didn't need any instructions. Geordie didn't have to say, 'Fasten the gate dear,' or 'Pick up m' stick will y'?' or 'Fetch a drop o' warm milk to get the lambs going again,' or 'Find me a pair of dry welly socks' . . . or anything like that. She would just do it anyway. They didn't chat much these days . . . didn't need to. Most times Doreen knew what Geordie was thinking long before he did.

By the time he got dried off and back to the shed, seven new lambs had been born. They were all alive and onto their pins. That was the good news.

The not so good news was they were all bleating and blaring and staggering about, creating total confusion. And worse . . . the pathetic, wet, wobbly wee things were followed wherever they went by a posse of crazy excited yowes, intent it seemed on butting them all to death. All that is, except one fanatical lady who was determined to claim *every* lamb as her very own. The noise was deafening! There were lost lambs looking for a mother, mothers searching for their children . . . and that brainless bugger mad keen to adopt everything!

Geordie caught *her* first. She was no more than a troublesome agitator, and he soon confirmed his suspicions that indeed she'd produced nowt but wind so far – and removed her from the equation altogether. The other four yowes, all displaying the clear and bloody signs of a recent 'happy event', he put into separate pens – and then began the tricky job of trying to match lambs to ewes.

That old four crop lady with half an ear missing, and half a horn, always had good strong dark faced lambs . . . patches of brown black wool about them . . . and there was just such a pair. Geordie offered them to 'half-lug', and she was immediately delighted. Right first time. Champion! Finding the correct parent for the rest of them wasn't so easy. It was a case of trial by rejection and elimination, but eventually three pairs were more or less settled and sucking, with the odd lamb being shuffled back and forth along the line. The unlucky little runt was battered straight out of contention by two ewes, and only warily, reluctantly considered by the third. Geordie figured she was actually the likeliest candidate, having the smallest lambs . . . *probably* triplets. They certainly looked like triplets. He pushed the pathetic thing in for a suck one more time, stood over the ewe, stick raised until the wretch found a tit, and then left him to get on with it. There were other jobs to do . . . other patients to keep alive. And the night had just begun.

CHAPTER TWO

At five o'clock Amanda Pratt from 'The Forge' came to help. Almost every evening she would jump down from the bus at the War Memorial stop, run home, dash straight upstairs to her room, and swap the neat high school uniform for her farming gear. Bright red wellies, patched jeans, chunky sweater and the Bon Jovi jacket were what she wore when working with 'Uncle George'. 'M' bonnie wee apprentice,' Geordie called her, and tried not to look too lecherously at this nymphet shepherdess, who always brightened up the lambing shed. Did fourteen-year-old girls always look like this, he wondered. Had he missed something when *he* was a youth? At that age Doreen was pretty enough, to be sure. Geordie thought she was a real cracker, and so did a few other lads. Oh aye, he'd had to use all his natural charm to catch Doreen Cowan. He used to call her D'reen baby . . . still did sometimes, when they were both in a good mood. It still made her laugh. But even then, the bonnie female package (as far as he could remember) bore little resemblance to this new well-contoured '90s model, with jet black pony tail swishing every time she tossed her head – and legs to her lugs. Of course young Amanda was a townie lass really, maybe *that* made a difference . . . the breeding, finer boned, more sophisticated upbringing perhaps. Certainly her mother was a smart tidy woman – nice smile. Her dad, on the other hand, looked as if he might've been the crit o' the litter. A good gust of wind would probably blow the man away, if he wasn't permanently attached to a briefcase. Aye, but those two had never really taken to country life. Seldom got involved with other village folk. Complained a lot about the lack of street lamps, and fortnightly garbage collections, and overflowing septic tanks, and having to travel ten miles to Safeways for a bag of muesli. Geordie suspected they might move back to 'civilisation' before too long. It wouldn't be the first time he'd seen the rural dream dissolve in daylight.

Amanda had fitted in much better. For a start she seemed to have an easy effortless relationship with animals. Not that soft, silly, cuddly approach the naive and uninitiated often have (well, maybe just a bit of that). But even on the first day she came over to the farm – you could tell she was a natural with animals. The dog liked her straight off. That was always a good sign, Geordie reckoned . . . Sweep didn't take to just anybody. And she hadn't been there more than an hour, when she was kickin' and swearin' at some awkward old yow. That was another promising signal he thought. As Geordie told his missus, 'The lass even *stands* in the right place. . . . I mean when you're shiftin' sheep up the road, or tryin' to persuade a daft bullock through a gateway . . . y' know, it's just ordinary shepherdin' stuff really, *we* take it for granted . . . but I think it's second nature to her as

8

well, like instinctive. Every other townie I've ever seen gets too close, or waves their arms about and makes a lot o' fuss . . . but Amanda knows exactly where to be . . .!' He was well impressed with that.

Geordie had been born at Glebe Farm sixty-eight years ago. His father had been the tenant before him, and his grandad before that. He knew every blade of grass, every thistle on the place . . . never wanted to be anywhere else. Wouldn't have been much good anywhere else. There wasn't a fortune to be made from 165 acres, he knew that – but Geordie didn't need a fortune. Maybe there wasn't anybody in the world who had 'enough' money (no matter how much they had) – but Geordie Dodds was about as close as you'd get. A grumbly content.

His only regret (and Doreen's too) – no kids. Sad . . . but they seldom talked about it now. Perhaps that's why he was so fond of Amanda.

Well, no doubt about it she was a gem, and more than just useful. Maybe hardly strong enough to turn a yow upside down, not yet . . . but a lot of the essential fiddly little jobs she could handle nicely now. In fact Geordie sometimes wondered how he'd ever managed before she came on the scene. She sprayed navels, stuffed pills down throats, encouraged dozy lambs to take that first important suck, bottle fed a hungry triplet, and marked the lambs as soon as they were dry enough, strong enough, to be moved out. Geordie had always numbered his newborn lambs with a paint stick. A pair of '2's, '3's, '4's, right through to '51's, or whatever. The singles would have a red spot on the tail head. Threes were lettered 'A's, 'B's, and 'C's. It was just his way of keeping a check on them all, he'd always done it. His father did the same – so it had to be right.

Just before dark Geordie and Amanda had a last careful look through the sheep out in the Marleyburn field. Sure,

9

some of the lambs weren't looking very happy, humpy-backed . . . but they'd hardly been dry for days – they were bound to look a bit depressed. Geordie noticed one lean yow making a fuss, bleating anxiously, looking about. She had a single lamb with her, but he didn't have the red spot on his bum, he was number 17. There had to be another 17 somewhere. Eventually Amanda and Sweep found him, lost and forlorn and hungry, all alone among some whin bushes at the far side. Maybe he'd been asleep when mother and brother moved off. Happily reunited he dived in for his supper, almost lifting his mother off her back legs. He would be alright, no problem, strong lamb.

In the cosiness of the shed, however, things were not entirely satisfactory. A canny four crop mule had produced twins, they were okay, already wobbling to their feet, while the ewe licked and nuzzled them into life. But over by the water trough an agitated gimmer (blue ear tag), a lady who hadn't yet experienced the joys of motherhood, was in a state of some confusion. She probably knew something extraordinary was happening, but what? Up and down, looking back, round and round, scratching in the straw, anxious, bewildered . . . and the big swollen head of a lamb hanging out under her tail. Geordie saw the goggly eyes, the fat blue tongue . . . no feet.

At the other end of the shed a third 'patient' was lying on her side pressing and straining and pushing for all she was worth. Amanda went over to take a closer look, and as the ewe got up, there it was – the bulbous red evidence of a prolapse . . . like a massive single rear light on a motorbike.

'Dammit!' was all Geordie said, and moved to deal with the gimmer before she strangled her lamb. God, it was barely two hours since he'd checked them.

The fella was only just alive, and his head had to go back where it came from for a start. Then there was some rearranging of legs to be done before he could be delivered. It took no more than ten minutes of experienced midwifery – but it was too late. Geordie blew into his mouth, pumped his legs and chest, swore and cursed . . . but to no avail. The lamb was dead. No blinking eye, no breath. He was enormous, surely a single. There would be no other surprises in there.

But mother had enough milk to feed the entire village, and Geordie decided to attempt a 'set-on'. It was always a bit risky with a flighty gimmer, but worth a try. He'd fed a pet for four days now, and it was becoming a bloody nuisance. Already he'd missed a couple of chances to get him 'mothered up'. Just too busy at the wrong time.

Amanda brought the eager orphan from the old stable, cradled in her arms, nibbling at her fingers. At least this lad would suck anything, there'd be no trouble on that score. Swiftly, expertly, Geordie had skinned the warm newborn body, and the bewildered pet was promptly stuffed into his second-hand suit, head and tail smeared with afterbirth, and pushed under mother's nose for consideration . . . approval . . . acceptance. Cautiously Geordie allowed the gimmer to get up. He knew she was as likely to jump a hurdle and flee into the night as stay with her new responsibilities . . . you could never tell. She was definitely edgy, but to Geordie's great relief she stayed. She even sniffed and licked and fussed. A little unsure perhaps, but at least she didn't kick the pet when he zoomed in. It *might* work. They put the family into a small private pen, away from other distractions, and hoped for the best.

By the time Geordie caught the prolapsed ewe, there was yet another beginning to lamb. They'd have to keep an eye on her, but first the operation. He'd done it 'a million' times . . . water in a bucket, lubrication, clean hands . . . gently push the scarlet mass back into the darkness . . . the daft yow trying to push it out again. . . . 'Relax y' silly bitch.' Clips to hopefully keep everything in place . . . a jab to discourage infection . . . fingers crossed. The patient seemed none the worse as she got up and shook herself. Geordie put a blue paint mark on her back . . . he'd have to watch out for this one when she eventually decided to lamb.

At nine o'clock Amanda went back to 'The Forge' – to boring maths homework, to dream of shepherding with Jon Bon Jovi. Not that she imagined for a moment he'd be any good with old mule yowes – but it might be quite exciting to teach him the tricks of the trade . . . in a dark lambing shed.

Geordie, alone again, stood and surveyed his flock for a while. The next lady on the agenda was probably half an hour away at least. He leaned on his hazel stick, hands under his chin, watching her. He didn't want to interfere in her private affairs at all – not if he could avoid it, not unless she needed some help. She looked as if she would manage alright. Time for a bite of supper perhaps. It was going to be another long session on the night shift, though . . . catch a little nap whenever y' get the chance . . . and just hope for no major problems before dawn.

He could never have guessed what fate had in store for him. . . .

CHAPTER THREE

The one place Gazza always felt comfortable, at ease, at home, was in the city. Anywhere in the city was okay. He knew his way around, where to get a decent pint, pick up a bird, get a ticket for St James's Park, collect the dole, find his mates ... cash the giro. What else did anybody need? Newcastle had a football team at last, there was the nightlife, the Bigg Market, the Quayside ... it was definitely the place to be. Plenty of action.

His grandad used to say, 'Get out o' town man, see a bit o' countryside – it's smashin'.' But as far as Gazza was concerned, you could keep your boring countryside. Countryside was nowt but grass and mad cows.

The first time he ever got off the Primrose estate, Mr Pringle the history teacher took the whole class to the Roman Wall. Jesus – what a drag! Just a pile o' stones in the middle of nowhere, and a lot of chat about some Italian geezer called Hadrian. It was just windy – and freezing cold! The journey home wasn't bad. A few of the lads had got some lager from somewhere. They were foolin' about in the back, and poor Wally was sick as a pig. Yeah, they had some laughs on the bus . . . but he'd never go back *there* again.

Whitley Bay was alright, at least on a weekend. He'd been down there a time or two. Serious drinkin', discos, amusement arcades, lasses on the 'tap'. The occasional punch-up on the Prom. Aye, Whitley could be a canny place on a Saturday night. If it wasn't rainin'.

When he first went out with Sharon, she'd dragged him out into the country one Sunday afternoon. He'd never forget it. He didn't really want to go. Leazes Park would've done, but he was pretty keen on her at the time, so he didn't argue too much. They took the little blue Nissan he had at the time, and parked up somewhere way beyond Rothbury. God, it was the end of the bloody world! Miles from anywhere . . . not a sound . . . except birds twitterin'.

She'd insisted on taking her scruffy little mongrel dog with them, and it had to have a walk of course . . . would've peed on the back seat if it hadn't. So they wandered for miles. Nothin'. Just trees and fields and a river. It was so quiet, Gazza hardly dare speak . . . and Sharon wasn't havin' any funny business either. She just blathered on about nature and rabbits, and all that stuff. Even picked flowers, took deep breaths, and kept sayin', 'Eeee, look at the view, innit luvley.'

What bleedin' view for Chrissake? There was nowt but hills and sheep and cows. Not a pub, or a café or a Safeways – or another human being in sight. It was those crazy cows that finally convinced Gazza he should've stayed at home.

There they were, walking though this field mindin' their own business – Sharon with that stupid mutt on a lead, in case he ran away and got lost in the wilderness – when suddenly there's a million cows right there in front of them. Big ones little ones, fat ones thin ones – like the cattle y' sometimes see on 'Bonanza'. Sharon said they were mothers with their calves. Gazza reckoned they were all bulls, but she said 'Rubbish,' and she seemed to know what she was talking about. 'Cows and calves,' she said. Her uncle Frank used to work on a farm once, so she had to be an 'expert' all of a sudden! Anyway this little bull or calf, or whatever, is lyin' havin' a kip right there beside the path, and the bloody dog starts barkin' at 'im, doesn't he. Wakes up the poor dozy thing, and 'calfie' starts blarin' for his mam. What a racket! You would think somebody was cuttin' his throat!

For a while they both thought this was very funny – just stood there laughin' while the mongrel yapped at the calf, and the calf shouted for his mother.

But that's when it all got a bit hairy. Suddenly, no warnin', this massive red and white monster comes gallopin' over the hill, full steam ahead . . . snortin' and slaverin' and howlin'. Smoke comin' out of her ears . . . headin' straight for them, tail in the air. This was mother in a right bad fettle, comin' to see what her little lad was cryin' about. . . . And if that wasn't bad enough – worse still . . . all the other cows, all her mates, they came too, all blarin' and shoutin,' and goin' at a hundred miles an hour!

The dog was petrified and tried to run away. But Sharon hung on t' the lead. She should've let the little sod go, of course – he would've sneaked through the hedge and escaped, or got mangled . . . one or the other. Who cares? As it was, they were *all* in a bother. . . . Had to run like hell and loup the fence . . . only just scrambled over in time. Only just! Gazza ripped his designer jeans on the barbed wire, Sharon was cryin' cos she'd sprained her ankle, the dog's havin' a fit, and the cows were still blarin' their heads off, tryin' to get through the hedge at the dog. It was bloody terrifyin'!

Gazza didn't feel right till he got back into Westgate Road. Alright, so Newcastle could be a bit rough at times, no argument about that – but there wasn't a big risk of being run over by a herd of stampedin' cattle, was there? Gazza *still* had sweaty nightmares about that day. . . . No kiddin'.

*   *   *

In what had once been the posh front parlour of No. 88 Armstrong Street, behind the plywood-covered bay window, Kevin, Sol, Wally and Gazza were planning the biggest robbery ever. It was so big, so daring, so dramatic – it might even push them into the major league. Give them 'real cred'. Whatever happened, they would surely become legends far beyond the Primrose estate. History was about to be made . . . and maybe a small fortune as well.

They met in a different empty house every time. Certainly there were plenty to choose from. The whole estate was little more than a wasteland of distressed derelict property now. Most of the windows were smashed, boarded up. Doors hanging by a hinge, or missing altogether. Broken glass, rubbish, bricks, and dead vehicles littering the pavements. You might walk the whole length of Armstrong Street or Stephenson Street from top to bottom, all the way down to the river, and still be hard pressed to find a house untouched . . . or anything resembling a traditional family unit living there. Today the old terraces were little more than rows of cheap hiding places, a shelter for a lot of 'no-hopers', druggies, teenage runaways (with two kids already) and an array of social misfits. Some of them maybe just unlucky – never had much of a chance . . . some who probably wouldn't fit anywhere. Once you were in there it certainly wasn't easy to get out.

For the kids, truancy was just a daily game of hide-and-seek, and at night gangs of scruffy little tearaways roamed in and out of the houses, pinching whatever they could get away with. They'd steal the telly while you went to take a leak during the adverts. Park a vehicle on the street, and it would be stripped, or completely gone within minutes. Even the sun seemed to avoid these streets. Far too dangerous.

On bad days it looked almost like a war zone. As if there had been a battle there . . . house to house fighting that had finally flushed out the solid hard-working respectable folk of yesterday. Now it seemed abandoned to mongrel dogs and scavengers and petty villains, to pick their way through the debris, and somehow survive on welfare or larceny – or both.

Occasionally a three-bedroom house would be advertised for no more than a couple of grand, and maybe some desperate unmarried mother or a couple trying to get a start might put the deposit down, and claim 'relief' . . . but few were prepared to take the risk. The 'chat' was that the heavy mob would eventually frighten everybody away, and buy up entire streets for 'washers'. Then they'd negotiate a massive redevelopment grant from the EEC and tart up the whole neighbourhood. Fountains and flowerbeds, plumbing and patios . . . and flog it off again at an enormous profit. Someday it might be the place to be . . . someday. . . . But if you were there already – that was hard to believe.

And yet, little more than a stone's throw away, across the Western Road, on the far side of Moor Park, behind the trees, was another world. House prices were quoted into six figures. M-reg. BMWs sat in the driveways. The residents had pension schemes, mortgages and foreign holidays . . . and viewed the Primrose people almost as an alien species. . . . And vice versa.

Of the four lads plotting in No. 88 only Sol had anything like a 'proper job'. For five nights a week he worked as a bouncer down at the club on the Quayside. Shaved head, earring, weight training, steroids . . . built like the proverbial brick privy – very few people argued with Sol. In a Saturday night punch-up, you'd want him on your side, that's for sure.

If asked, Kev would call himself a 'handyman', and fair enough he had a natural lazy talent to fix most things. He mended washing machines, installed central heating systems, rewired kitchens . . . and stole motorcars. Kev could do just about anything when moved . . . which was usually when broke and out of beer money – or maybe drug money . . . who knows? A neat guy, Kev . . . easy going – lived with a succession of glamorous girlfriends at the bottom end of Dunstan Avenue . . . top floor flat. Nice view over the city . . . not bad.

Wally was just a 'waster' really . . . more or less a full-time thief . . . and quite proud of it. Well what else was there to do? Y' had to have money . . . the giro was no use. Sometimes called Weasel, he was a slight wiry bloke with a narrow face, big sharp nose, and eyes that darted hither and thither . . . on the lookout for trouble. He didn't need to bother – trouble usually found him readily enough. He'd worked for a week in the canteen at Swan Hunters, but that was long ago, and he never found anything else that was suitable. You couldn't blame him – he didn't fancy a career washing dishes at Gosforth Park, or cleaning out the toilets at the Central Station, did he? And that was about all he was qualified for really.

He'd served two years in Durham already . . . he was well enough qualified for that. Being locked up was easy . . . good food and a telly. The last time the judge sent him down for six months. 'Nea bother yer honour,' said Wally, grinning like a fool from the dock. 'I can do that standin' on m' head. . . .'

His Honour hadn't been amused. 'In that case,' he said, 'we'd better make it *nine* months . . . it'll give you more time to get back on your feet!'

That was Wally all over . . . couldn't keep his mouth shut . . . just got in deeper.

Gazza Gallacher lived with sister Val and her current boyfriend in No. 27. Had a big room to himself, shared the housekeeping and the tacky bathroom. He'd once succumbed to a YOP programme, but luckily nothing came of that. He'd never been keen to work, not really. It tied y' down, didn't it? And after a·couple of burglaries with his Uncle Jackie, thievin' seemed a perfectly natural way to make a livin'. . . . You could lie-a-bed till noon, wander down to the Strawberry for a few jars . . . and just do a nice little job whenever the cash got low. He'd never been caught. Oh yes, questioned sometimes . . . the law was pretty sure he was up to no good, especially with Jackie's record, but nowt ever came of it. His proper name was Garry, but he looked a bit like the famous football star, depending on what hairstyle he favoured – and there was that same cocky confident air about him that appealed to the lasses. He usually had a bob or two to spend as well. That helped.

Come to think of it, his auld man never had a job either. Young Gazza was second generation dole queue . . . so were most of his pals, and both brothers. They'd never seen Dad get up and go to work with a bait bag over his shoulder. Mr Gallacher spent his life in the Comrades and the bookie's. . . . And mother? Well, she played bingo two nights a week, and somehow kept the house together. Not much of a family really – but sometimes they all gathered for tea on a Sunday, and Mam got out her best 'T-bone china'.

Sister Rose had a job of sorts at the Co-op, but she'd moved out long ago . . . shacked up with a mechanic called Wayne, a right plonker. They had a flat in Heaton now, gone all superior . . . microwave oven, and an L-reg. Fiesta with a stupid bear danglin' in the back window. She'd get pregnant likely . . . produce a load of smelly kids with dummies in their mouths. God, what a thought!

Anyway, that had nowt to do with Gazza. With this big business coming up, he'd assumed the role of leader, organiser. It was his idea, he was the boss on this one, the brains. It could be massive, and if they planned it right, it would be a doddle.

The idea came to him one wet afternoon while watching an old western on the telly (nicked of course, in a smash and grab from the Eldon Shopping Centre). The baddies had ridden into Deadwood, shot the fat old sheriff, robbed the bank, the saloon and the mayor's office. They'd grabbed some horses from the livery stable, a barrel of booze and two dancing girls from Ma Prentice's whore house, loaded up the wagon . . . and galloped off into the desert. Fantastic! Gazza saw himself immediately in the evil Jack Pallance role, and practised a cold sinister smile and a quick draw into the full-length mirror (part of a very nice house robbery in Wickham).

But what really appealed to him was the scene where the whole gang, all four of them, just walked down the main street. They were spread out across the road – in broad daylight, drinkin' and smokin' and laughin' . . . and shootin' in the air. Nobody dared do a thing about it. The town folk were all cowering in doorways, or hiding under the floor boards. It was great!

Of course Burt Lancaster, or somebody like that, killed them all in the end, but served them right really. They were pretty stupid . . . fast asleep round the campfire, when Burt crept up and shot them. Gazza would never be caught like that. The planning would be perfect. No errors.

'Right then bonnie lads – the first thing we've got t' do', said Gazza, 'is kill all the telephones. We'll want two or three hours to clean out that little village, and what we don't need is some daft old bat callin' in the coppers before we're finished.'

The other three nodded in agreement. 'So Kev cuts the phone lines at half-past twelve exactly. Nobody's gonna report a fault for hours, and it'll take BT most of the next day to fix it anyway. Alright?'

'Nea bother, man,' said Kevin. 'Where's the map?' They'd been on several 'reccies' through the village already. He just wanted to get the layout into his mind again. He and Gazza had even gone into the village pub for a quick pint and a packet of crisps. Nobody gave them a second glance. What's more they rarely met another vehicle on those country roads, and most nights after about eleven o'clock the whole area was fast asleep . . . lights out. All except that farmer's shed . . . like Blackpool illuminations – but he'd be no trouble.

The OS map was laid out on the carpet (stolen from a discount warehouse south of the river), cans of Newcastle Brown were brought from the fridge (taken from a downstairs flat in Jesmond) and Gazza eased himself into the three-seater sofa (late of a very substantial detached residence in Gosforth).

'There's half a dozen places I definitely want to hit between twelve-thirty and four, at the latest,' he said calmly. 'About three hours to get in, clean up, and bugger off. There's a fortune sitting there just waiting to be nicked. . . .'

Wally, however, wasn't entirely convinced . . . not yet. 'Are y' sure about this, like,' he asked, 'I mean it's just some crumby little village, miles from anywhere . . . hardly

anybody lives there, nuthin' happens, the place is dead. . . .
We've seen it!'

'Exactly,' said Gazza, sounding really cool. 'That's the
whole point isn't it. There'll be no aggro, no hassle. We'll
take the whole town over for the night . . . we'll wipe it
out!'

'*The whole town*,' exclaimed Wally. '*The whole town* . . .
what 'ya mean the whole town? There's only about seven
houses and a pub. It's hardly a town, is it? It's just a dozy
little dump, that's all. . . .'

Sol and Kev looked at Gazza, waiting for him to explain
again.

'Look,' he said patiently, 'we've been through all this
before, a hundred times. The trouble with thievin' in the city
is it's too bloody dangerous now – it's too busy . . . too many
nosy people about. Sooner or later somebody sees y', recog-
nises y'. There's a panda car round every corner, neighbourhood watch schemes on the posh estates . . . even surveillance
cameras. Christ man, there's somebody watchin' every time y'
blow your nose these days. It's gettin' impossible to steal in
peace! We've gotta get out o' town!'

He paused to take another swig of 'Broon'. 'Which
brings us to the real important thing – y' know where the
big money is now?' He waited, but not long enough for
anyone to butt in. 'Well I'll tell y' . . . it's out there in the
back o' beyond, that's where it is. It's in little God-forsaken
dead-end places like Hindburn!'

'Bollocks,' said Wally. 'The real rich folk live over on t'
other side of the park . . . Meadowgrove, Larkspur Gardens,
Holly Avenue – them places, always have done. It's rotten
wi' solicitors, accountants and fat company directors . . .
Gas Board, Northumbria Water, that sort. Y' can tell by the
big houses, fancy cars, bonnie gardens. Everybody knows
that. . . .'

'I'm not arguin'.' Gazza went to visit the fridge again. 'But like I say – it's gettin' more and more difficult man, too chancy. And believe me, Wally m' lad – the countryside is *heavin*' wi' money!'

'It's full o' hicks chewin' on straw, and whittlin' bits o' stick,' said Wally. 'They're just peasants, they've got nowt 'cept a pair o' wellies and a few sheep 'n' cows. I'm not stealin' sheep. I'm not that desperate . . . I'm not a bloody rustler!'

Gazza was becoming irritated. 'Jesus, have y' not been listenin' to what I've been tellin' y' for the last couple of weeks? Times have changed man. Your lawyers and fat cat directors are all in the country now. They're the only ones who can afford to *live* there! Hell's bells Wally, we're not gonna rob the peasants and steal their smelly old sheep y' fool. We're goin' for the big lads . . . and we'll be gone before anybody knows it. A piece o' cake.'

'Easy,' said Sol, grinning and cracking his knuckles ('love' on the fingers of the left hand, 'hate' on the right . . . a serpent disappearing up his arm into the sweatshirt).

'There might not be much in the Post Office,' Kev said, looking up from the map. 'Little spot like that . . . I'm surprised it's still there. Not many village Post Offices still operatin' these days. . . .'

Gazza didn't want any more negatives on his plan. 'Don't you believe it,' he said firmly. 'Every old sod for miles around collects the pension at that shop . . . and there'll be a load of stuff from the "Social", not t' mention stamps and postal orders 'n' that!' He was warming up. 'Then there's the Hall . . . just one old dame in there, surrounded by silver spoons and old masters. . . .'

'What old masters?' Sol asked, puzzled. 'How many gadgies *are* there in that place really. Is it a retirement home or somethin'?'

23

'They're valuable pictures, y' dummy, priceless works of art, worth a fortune man.' Gazza tossed Sol a can, and some beer bubbled out onto his lap when he ripped it open. 'Benny says he'll take anything we get, he'll pay a good price. . . .'

Kev was still engrossed in the map. 'Are we gonna do *every* house in the village?' he asked. 'All of them?'

'Maybe not *all* of them,' Gazza grinned. 'But definitely the best ones, where the high rollers live. The ones with two cars and a pony. . . .'

'All the money'll be in a bank somewhere.' Wally still wasn't sure . . . still moaning.

'Listen,' said Gazza, 'if we do this job right, I promise you it'll set us up for a twelve-month. We'll fill a couple o' vans in one night, and take it easy for the rest of the year. Lie low.' They were listening. 'And there's plenty more villages like this one y' know. I reckon we could be real trendsetters here . . . the first villains t' think of it!'

'Who else knows about this plan?' asked Wally.

'*Nobody*,' growled Gazza. 'Remember that, *nobody*! I had a chat with Benny, but he *has* to be in on it. He'll move the pictures and the antique stuff. We need Benny, he's got the connections . . . but that's as far as it goes. Understood?'

'Understood boss,' said Sol, and gave a sloppy mock salute. He was on his fifth pint – but it had no effect. He looked at his watch. He'd promised to visit his Mam tonight in Cramlington . . . 'bit borin', but she liked to see him once a week. Y' had to look after yer Mam, didn't y'?

'Motors?' Kev wanted to know. 'What do we need?'

'Two big vans,' said Gazza, 'to carry a ton at least, a bit o' power, double doors at the back, low platform so we can walk straight in. Maybe somethin' like a VW Transporter, or a good Ford Transit would do nicely. . . .'

'Does the colour matter?'

'Not really, we can soon spray it, change the plates. We'll need to put the logo on one of them. Can y' do it?'

'Oh aye,' said Kev, as if it was an item on a shopping list. 'Just tell us when.'

Wally still wasn't really happy. 'What happens if we come up agin any aggro?' he asked. 'I mean there might be some auld general with a sword and a Rottweiler, who thinks he's still at Waterloo. . . .'

'He'll not be much trouble if he *was* at Waterloo,' Gazza grinned, 'that's for sure. But I think you're right – we should be tooled up just in case . . . just to put the frighteners on if we come across a local hero!'

'Y' mean guns?' Wally wasn't in favour of guns.

'Yea, I think we need a sawn-off job. It'll look business-like if some idiot comes downstairs waving a cricket bat. . . . And it always speeds things up as well . . . frightens them t' death. . . .'

'Would y' shoot somebody like?' Wally asked, staring anxiously at his leader.

'Depends,' said Gazza.

'What y' mean, depends . . . depends on what? Like if he doesn't smile nicely or somethin' . . .?'

'Don't be daft, of course not. But if it comes down to him or me . . . it's gotta be him, hasn't it?'

'Or her?' asked Wally quietly.

Gazza didn't answer that one, perhaps he didn't hear. He turned to Sol. 'Can you deal with it Sol? You'll see Victor tonight, go to a couple o' hundred for the right piece . . . we can always move it on later – okay?'

'So *when*?' asked Kev. 'When do we go?'

'Next Monday night,' said Gazza. 'The 25th.' He'd given this some very careful thought. It was all part of the master plan. Nothing left to chance. The weekend was no good. People tended to go out Friday and Saturday nights. They came home late, or had friends in, who *left* late. Same thing. Too many cars on the roads, even in the early hours. And Wednesday was out . . . generally something going on late at the pub. He'd discovered this on two of the 'reccies'. A lock-in after a darts match he thought. Lights still blazing at 11.30. And of course Sol was on duty at the club every night bar Sunday and Monday, so that restricted the choice a bit. They definitely needed Sol on the team. So how about Sunday? No, Gazza wasn't too happy about Sunday. Not for any religious reasons you understand. No, it was the Post Office that worried him on a Sunday. Well, let's face it – they wouldn't have cash lying about in there all weekend, would they? But on Monday morning, well now, they'd have to be geared up for all the 'crumblies'. Pensions and sick notes to be cashed through the week. Gazza reckoned there had to be a Securicor delivery early Monday morning sometime.

And another thing. He figured people were often feeling pretty low on a Monday night . . . first day back at work again wasn't it? Back into that boring routine . . . knackered, nowt on the telly . . . early to bed. Once he'd done a dummy run late on a Monday night, driven slowly through the village, stopped for a fag up the road somewhere . . . watching for signs of life. Nothing, dead, lights out. . . . Well, all except for that farm shed, and some miserable sheep bleating. But he hardly anticipated much bother from a flock of scabby old sheep.

Yea, next Monday was definitely the night to go. The decision was made. You could plan and organise till Gateshead won the Premiership – but sooner or later you just had to do it!

Gazza got up from the sofa. He was meeting Sharon in half an hour. To the 'Warner', and then on for an Indian. He was looking forward to a session with Sharon, hadn't seen her for three days . . . withdrawal symptoms creeping up on 'im. He could feel them. He must be gettin' serious about this lass. If this caper went according to plan, it could set them up nicely. Maybe even get them off the Primrose estate into a canny little flat somewhere decent. That might not be such a bad idea. . . .

'So get the transport organised,' he said to Kev. 'And don't forget the gun Sol . . . we're goin' for broke on Monday night. Alright?'

Outside three scruffy tearaways in holey jeans, dirty Newcastle United shirts, and multicoloured trainers . . . barely into their teens, but with old-fashioned faces . . . were 'minding' the Granada. (Twenty-five quid, MOT failure . . . Kev had got it going like a bird.) Gazza was pleased to see all the wheels still attached, the seats and radio still in place. So the kids were running a little protection racket already, so what? It was well worth it. He could afford the fiver. Next week he would be buying a *decent* motor . . . just wait. In fact he should dump the Granada this weekend. Burn it.

He was stuck at the traffic lights in the Haymarket when he opened the glove compartment, and discovered twenty fags and his 'gold' lighter were missing. Bloody kids!

CHAPTER FOUR

This was a stressful time for Trevor Pratt. On the frantic run up to April 5th, the lights at Drew Pratt and Illingworth would burn far into the night, as clients' accounts were shuffled and juggled through their final 'creative lap' to the year end. Balance sheets to keep shareholders happy, balance sheets to keep creditors at bay, balance sheets to appease the Inland Revenue, mollify the bank, confuse the predator. Balance sheets designed to be mystifying and impenetrable . . . to everyone bar Trevor. . . .

The job came home to Hindburn with him at this time of year. A couple of large gin 'n' tonics, a light supper – and Trevor would disappear into his private den at the end of the passage, there to conjure and contrive. It wasn't easy to stay awake, let alone be alert and professionally devious. Sometimes Celia would float in with coffee, twitter for a while, and leave him wondering if he'd included the capital gains allowance in the current equation. . . . Maybe it was in there *twice* now. Start again.

Daughter Tabatha banged violently on the door and shouted, 'Night Daddy,' from the other side. He heard her hooves galloping up the stairs, and prancing about the bedroom overhead . . . the cassette player bursting into life. That threw him as well. He'd been in the middle of a tricky account, trying desperately to conceal a major slice of profit . . . punching figures on the calculator . . . and now the six digits displayed there meant absolutely nothing. He couldn't remember how he'd arrived at them.

When Amanda crashed in unannounced, and kissed him on the top of his balding pate, he abandoned ship altogether. His brain slipped out of gear. He pressed the 'off' button on the adding machine, and resigned himself to a 'devoted Daddy' programme.

There were three women in his life now . . . well the girls were *almost* women . . . all apparently convinced he was a financial genius. Indeed he wished he *was.* . . . They certainly had a prodigious talent for spending whatever he made. The house was awash with chic dresses and fashionable footwear. He was quite astonished how many pairs of shoes six female feet required. And now the entire house seemed to be 'decorated' with bras. They were everywhere! Bathrooms and bedrooms were cluttered with sophisticated potions and lotions in cleverly designed expensive jars. The washing machine was in a constant state of agitation, the phone seldom silent. There were earnest giggly girlie conversations 'twixt mother and daughter, on the stairs, in the kitchen, behind half-closed doors. A conspiracy? Probably not, but it seemed all they had to do was whisper seductively into Daddy's ear, and wait for the cash to appear, as if by magic. The poor man was outnumbered . . . and often out-manoeuvred!

Then there was Tabatha's horse. Just a pony really, but fourteen hands of mobile incinerator. It cost a damned fortune to keep! There was never a blade of grass in the croft throughout the whole year. The 1.6 acres were mostly nettles, dockens and thistles anyway – but that pompous little beast wouldn't eat them. The colour of his 'estate' changed only slowly, as the seasons came and went. A pale unenthusiastic green in spring, gradually fading to yellow, then brown, until finally November's rains rendered it akin to the Somme. At that time poor Dessie had to be brought in to shelter in the new wooden stable for the rest of the winter. More expenditure on pony nuts and small bales of hay and bedding straw bought from Mr Dodds or Sep Robson, at Clartiehole – right through to April. And what about all the horsey equipment . . . saddles, bridles, martingale (whatever that was), jodhpurs, hard hat, hacking jacket, boots. There was no end to it. But as Celia constantly reminded him, 'You wouldn't want your daughter to feel ashamed at the Pony Club, would you dear?'

Nevertheless, he sometimes thought a little mild humiliation wouldn't do the young lady any harm . . . and it would certainly be cheaper!

At least Amanda had come out of the gee-gee phase. He had to be thankful for that. For a year or two it had been *double* everything, and the household chat had revolved solely round withers and fetlocks and eventing. But, at last, thank the Lord, almost overnight Amanda had grown up, and out, and round – and a ravenous gelding called Rummy had been discarded. That was the good news. But a growing army of spotty youths yomping out from town every weekend, no doubt intent on deflowering his eldest daughter, had him distinctly worried. He hoped Celia had delivered the necessary warnings. The last thing he needed was a nasty little surprise!

Someday, Trevor supposed, the girls would eventually be married. Heaven knows how much that would cost. His partner Harry Illingworth had recently spent about ten grand on *his* daughter's nuptials. Posh reception, vast tent on the lawn, endless supplies of 'champers', salmon, strawberries ... even a jazz band. It was an alarming prospect. *Two* alarming prospects in fact! Maybe he should have taken out some sort of insurance as soon as they were born – but you seldom have the spare cash, or the spare vision at that stage, do you? And in any case such a policy would probably only run to a few bottles of plonk, and a take-away pizza by the time it eventually matured.

At least the girls were pretty, everybody said so, and you had to be grateful for that. Well, it seemed reasonable to suppose *someone* would take them off his hands, sooner or later. Early days, of course, but already he envisaged Amanda being charmed out of her wellies by some gentleman farmer with a wheat mountain. He wasn't at all sure what constituted a gentleman farmer, in fact the very expression appeared to be a contradiction ... but certainly any *poor* hard-working peasant wouldn't do. ... No matter how attractive his other rural assets might be, Amanda's man would have to own a nice big Georgian farmhouse, set in rolling parkland. Perhaps the west wing could accommodate Trevor and Celia in their twilight years – rent-free, naturally. He saw acres and acres, or was it hectares and hectares? (Somehow hectares never sounded quite so impressive.) Anyway, lots of corn waving in the breeze, and some cows would be nice. No matter what anybody said about BSE, he liked cows. Not so sure about sheep ... smelly things. In fact he could smell them now on Amanda's sweater as she sat there on his lap. At least he assumed that's what it was. It surely wasn't something sophisticated and French from one of those expensive bottles in the bathroom ... was it?

. . . And Tabatha? Well at the moment she was still in love with Dessie. Maybe she'd get over it. . . . If not, then the Aga Khan might be a suitable suitor, or Sheik Mohammed . . . or at worst, an embryo MFH. Whoever it might be, somebody with a gee-gee was a hot favourite at this stage. Meanwhile he was stuck with them. . . . What a pair . . . one reeked of mule yow, and the other smelled like a sweaty steeplechaser. If that didn't inhibit prospective husbands, he wondered what would. . . .

Amanda dragged him back to the here and now. 'Soopah time down at the farm, Daddy,' she said. 'Absolutely fascinating. George was quite magnificent – he's simply a genius with sheep.'

'Really?' Trevor said, trying to smile and be enthusiastic.

'We lost a muckle hanged single though,' Amanda went on. 'Enormous – poor thing choked t' death. George had to skin 'im and set on a spare.'

'Muckle hanged single,' Trevor repeated slowly and deliberately. 'What on earth is a muckle hanged single, for heaven's sake?'

Amanda was obliged to explain about presentation at birth – ideally two front legs and the head, but in this case only a head. It meant trouble, swollen tongue, strangulation. It all sounded very messy and uncomfortable, and there were words he wasn't sure young ladies should be using.

'We had a back-body out as well!' she exclaimed, as if it was a winning lottery ticket.

'I hardly dare ask,' said Trevor. 'Don't tell me – the lamb came into the world tail first . . .?'

'Good Lord no,' she said almost contemptuously. 'The poor ewe simply pushed her cervix out . . . we had to put it back again, and stitch up her vulva . . .!'

'Oh my God!' Trevor was totally embarrassed, confused,

out of his depth. 'I don't think I want to hear any more of this,' he groaned.

'It's perfectly normal,' said Amanda calmly, 'it happens all the time. George is teaching me everything, and the sheep are lovely. We've only lost five lambs so far . . . oh, and a dead ewe . . . pneumonia I think . . . but to be fair there's another with a bad case of mastitis. She has one deaf tit . . . she might not survive. . . .'

'One deaf tit?' Trevor exclaimed. 'What the hell's going on over there. I think you should go to bed and read Enid Blyton or Winnie the Pooh!' He gave her a kiss and a squeeze, and shooed her out of the office. 'And have a bath,' he shouted as she went out the door, 'you smell quite revolting!'

Trevor tried to go back to his work, but couldn't concentrate. He heard the shower upstairs, and something he assumed to be pop music still coming from Tabatha's room. He went through to the lounge where Celia was asleep with Jeremy Paxman. He was insulting a stuttering politician, determined not to answer any questions. Celia lay sprawled on the sofa, eyes closed, mouth open . . . an occasional subdued squeak, a twitch, the suspicions of a smile. Butch the labrador did much the same sort of thing when *he* was dreaming – but it seemed unlikely Mrs P. was chasing rabbits.

He decided to take the dog for a walk. The rain had almost stopped. He might stroll up to Hindhope and back, or even round the block by the Clartiehole Road. It was only a couple of miles . . . it would clear the arithmetic from his head.

The lights were still shining in the shed at the Glebe Farm as he turned left into the village . . . Mr Dodds presumably still performing complicated obstetrics on his unfortunate animals.

Over the road, the White Hart was still very much awake

too – several vehicles parked there, the sounds of chatter and clinking glasses still filtered out into the night, well after 'last orders'.

For a week or two, when they first moved into the village, Trevor and Celia had walked over to the pub for early evening drinks; sometimes they even stayed for a bar meal. He told the staff at work how delightful his local was, so friendly, full of real characters. But to be honest he had never been entirely comfortable in there. All that obscure agricultural chat was beyond his comprehension . . . the gimmer trade, the price of store cattle, the weather. God, they were always discussing and analysing the weather . . . all of them 'expert' forecasters. No, he didn't really fit, he knew that. The natives were friendly enough – somebody nearly always muttered, 'Canny night,' or 'How are y' Mister Pratt?' But the crack, and the sudden bursts of laugher, seldom included him. He would look up, turn round and smile, but was rarely in on the joke. He probably wouldn't understand it anyway. Yes, there was definitely a divide . . . the old locals and the newcomers . . . them and us. Never spelled out, nothing unpleasant – but it was still there in the air, he thought.

After a while Celia didn't want to go at all. She said she always felt uncomfortable, and thought the White Hart wasn't entirely at ease with her either. Often she would be the only woman in the place. Trevor went less and less, and then only to get out of the house. Now they occasionally went to the Queens instead, had cocktails in the sepulchral lounge bar, and a bottle of nice wine with dinner. That was more their scene. The Beedays from Hindhope were often in on a Friday night, Donald and Diana Peabody who lived at Paddock House, were regulars . . . and the head waiter always recognised them now.

Trevor walked on past the trees on the corner, dark,

silent, shadowed – but for the last couple of days the noisy rooks had begun building their high-rise homes. The merest suspicion of spring perhaps, in spite of the weather.

Peter Foggin's garage was in darkness too, the three pumps standing silently to attention on the forecourt. One upstairs light through blue curtains at the house. Daisy Foggin reading in bed perhaps, waiting for Peter to come home from the pub next door. That's where he'd be, right enough. Two pints every night, no more no less . . . and a game of dominoes with Tommy Cleghorn, 10p a game. . . . High rollers.

Trevor was becoming used to the dark now – he could see the dim shape of Butch twenty yards ahead, investigating interesting smells in the bottom of the hedge, and peeing at regular intervals. He passed the silhouette of the Dawson house on the right, no lights there . . . the 'For Sale' sign standing starkly by the road. He heard the high-pitched bleating of a lamb somewhere in the black distance – and was that the deeper throaty sound of mother answering? He supposed it was.

On the left Gloria Swanson's cottage. There were still lights on in there, curtains drawn, nothing to see. Did he hear a little music, a little laughter? An intimate party for two perhaps? Gloria seldom spent the night alone it seemed, and sure enough there was another car in the drive – a black Ford Mondeo. He'd heard the local lads discussing the lady's sex life in the pub many a time . . . or at least what they imagined went on. Geordie Dodds said she reminded him of a Land Army lass he fancied long ago . . . before he met Doreen of course.

Certainly Gloria was a very attractive woman, and she knew it. Forty maybe, and still with a really smart figure. Good legs, long brown hair – and nearly always a saucy smile that suggested she was thinking about something outrageous, something she knew but you didn't. She dressed nicely too − except on hot summer days, when she *un*dressed nicely. Trevor had seen her sunbathing topless last year. Her back garden could be viewed easily from the Pratt's bathroom . . . if he stood tiptoe on the loo seat, hung on to the shower rail, and peeped out at the top left-hand corner of the little frosted window.

Mr Pratt and his dog walked over the bridge that spanned the Marleyburn, and up the rise to Haugh House, where Giles and Polly Pollock lived. Giles was seldom at home these days, but Celia had seen him at the Post Office only yesterday. Nobody was sure what the man did now, but he appeared to have unlimited funds . . . quite seriously rich . . . cars, villas, even a boat somewhere, they said. The man had obviously done extremely well when he sold his stake in Applepeel Electronics. There had been a few rumblings of insider trading, and Giles had even spent a night in custody − but it never came to anything. Of course he was in the big league, and the big league didn't often get done for their corporate shenanigans. It was the poor little accountants who innocently rearranged a few quid in the client account who ended up in chains!

Headlights were approaching slowly from the village . . . maybe the late drinkers were leaving the White Hart. Trevor called Butch to heel, and backed into the hedge. A few seconds later a dark coloured van glided gently past, tail lights blinking as it went beyond the trees, and up towards Hindhope. He thought it turned left there, but when asked about it later, he couldn't be sure. Certainly when he got to the top of the hill, there was no sign of it.

He himself turned left at the old farm, and walked briskly down to the bottom road, aware of the stillness of the countryside at night. He arrived back home around midnight. Butch took a final sniff at the night, and crept away into his box. The pub was silent at last, only a dim light in the bar, where Jack was probably collecting glasses and emptying ashtrays. The maternity unit at the Glebe Farm was quiet too, but still a blaze of light. They said Mr Dodds sometimes slept in there on the straw bales – never went to bed.

Trevor wondered if Gloria was tucked up with 'Mondeo man'. A host of interesting images danced through his head. Like pictures from an early flickering black-and-white movie, in which the dark mustachioed villain chases the demure heroine round and round the bedroom . . . both of them over-acting like mad – the pianist desperately trying to keep pace.

He reluctantly switched off his imagination, and went to bed. Celia was dreaming again, and still twitching like a dormant labrador.

*   *   *

Geordie Dodds, standing at the back door with a cigarette and a mug of tea, saw the lights go out at 'The Forge' . . . and wearily wandered over the yard to check his sheep again. A vehicle came slowly down the village from the Haugh House end, lights on dip. It must be somebody local. Who else would be on this road at this time of night! And showing a little consideration as well, that was nice. Not like the young tearaways who came blasting through Hindburn in the early hours most weekends – lights blazing, as if they were leading the Lombard Rally.

In the shed most of the ewes were quiet, lying about on the clean straw, eyes half closed, jaws grinding. A four crop mule (red ear tag) got up, scratched the bedding with a front foot, performed a pirouette, and lay down again. He checked those who had lambed earlier – the births he'd had to sort out, and the set-on pet with the gimmer. He was lying on his foster mother's back, in his smelly over-sized coat, apparently as full as an egg . . . almost grinning.

Geordie decided he could grab an hour's kip by the kitchen fire before the next inspection. God, he was tired. Not that he didn't enjoy lambing most of the time . . . he did. In fact if y' got any luck at all, and some decent weather, it could be the most satisfying job on earth . . . no question. But this year had been really hard work, just trying to keep everything alive. Young lambs didn't like being wet all the time . . . who did?

He opened his little black note book and completed the audit for the day . . . with a little chewed pencil two inches long. Nine twins, two singles and a three born in the last twenty-four hours. Fifty-one ewes left out of a hundred and twenty-two . . . past half way. It hadn't been easy, but so far so good.

He stretched and yawned, and pushed his feet nearer the fire. He assumed he was probably the only person in the village not a-bed. He was wrong of course.

CHAPTER FIVE

When Gazza and Kev walked boldly into the White Hart three weeks before the robbery, nobody had taken a blind bit of notice. The dour dark bloke behind the bar, shirt sleeves rolled up, substantial belly hidden below the counter, hadn't even spoken. He just looked more or less in their general direction, and only pulled *their* pints after all his regulars had been served. Arrogant sod.

They found a seat by the door, a long way from the fire. It was canny beer though. Kev said so, as he wiped the froth from his top lip with the back of his hand. There was a posh end through behind the bar, marked 'Lounge', but nobody was in there. No light, no Leek Club committee meeting tonight. Not much passing trade at this time of year. No need for any extra expensive heating.

There were perhaps a dozen people in the 'cosy' end, all male. Nobody wore a suit or a tie. Some even had mucky overalls — straight from work maybe . . . wagon drivers, farmers. Most of them kept their caps on. There were a couple of sticks hanging on the back of the door. About half the customers were smokers, and at least three pipe men enveloped in clouds from Condor Bar. And they were all talking at once, or so it seemed. Occasionally even mine host became quite animated, especially when the chat got round to football. 'Kevin Keegan? I wouldn't give that fella the time o' day . . .!' he snarled.

Gazza wanted to join in, but thought better of it. Wiser just to have a quiet drink, keep yer head down, listen . . . look the place over. That's what they were here for. . . .

Snippets of conversation and argument filtered through from the smoky fog, punctuated sometimes by howls of laughter, cries of disbelief, frequent expletives, banging of glasses. A voice insisting to be heard, chatter rising and falling but never still. The two townie lads didn't really have a clue what it was all about. Strange words in a different Geordie dialect. Here they were no more than half an hour from Newcastle, and it was another ruddy language!

The men were talking seriously, while contemplating subtle domino moves. 'Are y' nearly finished the lambin' then?'

'Forty-seven t' go . . . three pairs and a pair o' threes last night. . . .'

'Plenty milk?'

'Well I wouldn't say that Charlie . . . it's hardly runnin' out o' them . . . cold east wind man . . .'

A double blank had them all knocking. It was a count. 'Were y' at the mart today?'

'Aye, canny trade. Somebody must have some grass somewhere. Alfie bought a few out-wintered bullocks off the North Moor . . . four-fifty a-piece, lean as crows. Mind they'll shift, they've definitely not been spoilt. . . .'

'So how's your rape lookin'?' a voice wanted to know.

'Patchy man – top dressed it last week, but the pigeons are givin' it hell!'

Short, sharp, agricultural exchanges. It might as well've been Swahili. What the hell were they talking about? Kev looked at Gazza, shrugged his shoulders, lit a cigarette and moved the Blue Star ashtray a little closer. A big bloke with a grin on his face went out through the door on his way to the gents – cocked his head as he passed, but said nothing.

'You'll have a wee nip afore y' go?' said a voice somewhere across by the bar. For a moment the lads thought it was directed at them – but of course it wasn't.

'No thanks, I better get back. . . . There's a cow calvin' . . .'

'Arthur's buyin',' somebody shouted, amid howls of laughter . . . 'he must've got his subsidy cheque. . . .'

More laughter, more smoke, more chatter. The noise reminded Gazza of a saloon in a cowboy film . . . except there was no pianist playing 'Yellow Rose of Texas', no dancing girls to sit on his knee, no copper spittoons . . . and as far as he could tell, no pistols . . . just sticks. These dumb yokels couldn't shoot a turnip at a dozen paces anyway. He drained his glass and nodded to Kev. Time to go. They hadn't been in this boring dive for more than ten minutes, but it was no place for a couple of suave city boys like them. City boys on the brink of the big league.

They climbed into the black Ford, wheeled it around, kicking up the car park gravel, and headed for the A1. They could see the glowing orange lights of Tyneside winking on the south-east horizon. Somewhere in among that lot was the Primrose estate. Okay, so it wasn't exactly Hollywood – but it was home.

In the Hart, Jack pulled pints of 'Special' for Arthur and Tommy Thompson, took a fiver and handed back some change. 'So what do y' make o' them two callants?' he asked, inclining his head towards the door. 'I wonder what brings them oot bye . . .?'

'Up t' no good, that's for sure,' said Tommy. 'They'll be sniffin' about for somethin' t' pinch likely. Somebody's car, or a farm Quad maybe . . . a few o' them missin' lately.'

'A couple o' right wasters,' Arthur reckoned.

Samuel Forsythe, still grinning, returned from his sortie across the yard, wiped his wellies on the mat, and found his half-full glass exactly where he'd left it. 'Write it down,' he said to the landlord, 'MCN 974H . . . black Granada, bit of a dent on the boot lid, and one sidelight not workin' . . . I think I've seen that car before. . . .'

'Poachers?' Jack suggested as he wiped the counter.

'No, I don't think so,' said Samuel, 'I canna see those lads plodgin' about after pheasants in the dark. . . . But they've definitely got somethin' on their minds. . . .'

* * *

Miss Angela Fenwicke-Browne of Hindburn Hall had seen the sinister black Granada as well. Half-past nine last Sunday night, coming home from a Hunt committee meeting at the Colonel's (only two dry sherries) and there it was – parked in a field gateway just down from the lodge – no lights. A courting couple, she'd assumed, at first – and being a well-bred conservative lady, she determined not to look too closely. All rather sordid these days, no shame. That was until she caught sight of the two shadowy male figures behind the car, facing into the hedge. They were obviously relieving themselves. Each appeared to have a can of lager, or some such beverage, in one hand, and . . . well . . . she simply refused to contemplate what might be in the other.

It was but a fleeting image of course. She was past, and had turned into the Hall driveway before she realised just what an incongruous pair they were. Even in the car head-lights it was clear one fellow was as big as a house, and his companion a mere runt. A little weasel of a man.

Miss Angela hadn't really given the incident much more thought. Good heavens she had far more important matters to worry about. Parish Council tomorrow, for a start. Then there was bridge on Tuesday evening, coffee with Mrs Peabody (Save the Badger) Thursday, shopping on Friday, and flowers for the church at the weekend. It was all go! It wasn't until the two charming young policemen drove up in their white van, while she was forking dandelions out of the lawn, that she remembered the urinating strangers.

'Oh yes, rather like Laurel and Hardy,' she said, 'A big one and a little one.'

'I can assure you, madam, these two are not comedians,' the sergeant said in a very grave voice. 'We've had reports of this vehicle in the vicinity on more than one occasion, and have reason to believe they *may* be planning some mischief. . . .'

'Mischief,' snorted Miss Angela. 'Mischief? There's nothing for them here officer. I never have any money these days, and in any case I'd set the dogs on them if the scoundrels came anywhere near . . .!'

This seemed to be the cue for two overweight border terriers to waddle down the steps from the front porch, and collapse on the grass. They didn't impress the sergeant as a serious deterrent, and he couldn't resist a sideways glance at his colleague. 'Quite,' he said. 'But if you'll forgive me Miss Fenwicke-Browne, you're no longer a young woman are you? – and we understand you live alone. There's no man on the premises, is there?'

'Don't need one,' snarled Miss Angela. 'Never did . . . just a damned nuisance . . . wouldn't have one in the house. I'd rather have a good dog any day . . .!'

The two policemen looked down, quite a long way down, to the plump little lady standing before them, hands

43

on hips, stout legs apart, leather brogues, stockings as thick as trousers, tweed skirt, Barbour jacket and navy-blue headscarf . . . and wondered just how tough she really was. Feisty was a word that occurred to the sergeant. He considered how old she might be, and suspected she'd looked just like this for the last forty years or more. A formidable old girl, no doubt about that. . . . But how would she cope with a pair of professional hooligans from the town, hell bent on relieving her of the family silver . . . ?

'You'll ring us if you see those men again, won't you madam?' he said. 'And on no account approach them yourself – they could be very dangerous.'

'So am I,' she growled – and attacked another dandelion with terrifying vigour.

*   *   *

Fred and Doris Little who ran the village shop were always pleased to see anybody, and when Kev and Gazza sauntered in one day, Doris smiled a friendly welcome as she always did. Whoever it might be – the Queen, Saddam Hussein or some destitute tramp – it would make no difference to them. It was just the way they were. It hadn't much to do with customer care, or the 'Citizen's Charter', or anything they might have read about in the Retailer's Handbook. They were just really canny folk. They couldn't help it.

Mind you, it wasn't getting any easier. A few years ago the business had been a good little earner – especially when you considered the accommodation over the shop. The Post Office licence was always the bread and butter of course, but they'd steadily expanded into what eventually became a handy little general store. Alright, hardly Tesco perhaps, but everybody round about knew if they ran out of life's absolute essentials, like tobacco, tea, toilet rolls, something quick 'n' easy for supper . . . Fred and Doris would have it tucked away on the crowded shelves, somewhere. And they were open all hours, every day of the week, even on a Sunday morning – if only for the papers. On that day the shop became a gathering place for a whole cross-section of rural society. The Colonel came to collect his *Sunday Times*, Freddie Fox QC took the *Independent*, Gloria Swanson, *News of the World* and the *Telegraph* (a combination that covered most things . . . or *un*covered them). Tommy Cleghorn and many others stuck to the local 'rag', if only to get a thoroughly biased report on Saturday's Newcastle match. On a fine sabbath morning they would linger and blather for hours. On wet days, they would mutter, 'What a terrible mornin' eh?' and hurry home for lunch.

The Colonel always said 'Morning,' in a loud voice to everyone, never quite sure who anybody was. Fred and Doris, on the other hand, knew *all* the names, as well as everyone's order. 'Ah, Mr Dodds, your *Mirror*, and anything else today . . . plenty baccie?'

'How are you Alice – the *Mail* . . . and a jar of marmalade – certainly.'

'Are you well Charlie? Lambing going alright? The *Sun* isn't it? Thank you very much. 'Bye.'

The pile of news and scandal eventually disappeared by noon, and the door was locked again till Monday.

Monday was always a good day for business. The Post Office was busy. People wrote letters and paid bills over the weekend. They needed stamps and postal orders. They came in with DSS booklets for pensions and benefits. They topped up the household shopping . . . items forgotten or consumed since Friday. Miss Angela was one of the few who bought *everything* there. 'A matter of principle,' she said. 'Support the village shop, or the damn thing will close – then you'll be sorry!'

But everyone knew it was only a matter of time. They

couldn't go on competing much longer. They couldn't indulge in 'loss leaders', 'special offers', and 'price wars'. It was a constant battle now just to keep their heads above water. Nobody's fault, nobody to blame . . . simply times that were a-changin'.

All the children went to school in town now, didn't they? – ferried there by elegant young mothers in four-wheel drive off-roaders that never saw a clart. By 9.30 am these ladies were parked free, driving a supermarket trolley, and helping themselves to Italian pizzas, Chilean wine, French paté or whatever. Seduced by easier, cheaper, warmer . . . all under one roof. Hair done at 'Creations', and coffee on the way home with Kate or Clarissa . . . lovely. Village shop? Who needs a village shop? Except perhaps in dire emergency. Mrs Beeday felt positively embarrassed on the rare occasions she was obliged to drop in for a jar of Maxwell House, or catch the evening post . . . and yet Fred and Doris would greet her in the same cheery fashion every time. It almost made it worse for poor Mrs Beeday.

It was the same with total strangers, tourists passing by – and when two scruffy lads they'd never seen before barged arrogantly and noisily through the door, late one afternoon, Doris chirped a merry 'Good day' as usual. They didn't answer. Where Gazza and Kev came from nobody said 'Good day' . . . it seldom was. Doris just got on with whatever she was doing, totting up the takings, writing little memos to order more butter, smoked ham, tinned tomatoes. They wandered round the shop, one hand in a pocket, picking up, putting back . . . poking about, eyes down. Just a touch of menace in the air. Doris kept an eye on them, pleased the grill at the Post Office was closed (last collection half an hour ago). Fred was making a pot of tea in the back. Eventually Gazza decided he should buy twenty cigarettes . . . and while he silently paid for them, Kev silently slipped a few bars of chocolate into his anorak pocket, still on the move, never looking up.

'Oh, and two cans of coke,' mumbled Gazza, turning back, fiddling with loose change. He could see Kev's head beyond the display of soup cans, and knew he'd be nicking something. Doris saw him too, but was disinclined to make anything of it. These boys were capable of wrecking the shop just for the hell of it – not to be trifled with. She had breathed a huge sigh of relief when they finally left, banging the door behind them. The bell almost coming off the wall, and perhaps it was the ringing that brought Fred out of the kitchen.

'Who was that?' he asked looking out of the shop window, as the car roared away.

'Dunno,' said Doris. 'Just passing through I think. . . .' She realised her hands were unsteady, and her heartbeat had gone up a notch. She needed that cup of tea. She didn't mention the chocolate bars.

* * *

Tommy Cleghorn saw them the same day.

Tommy was a gardener . . . good enough at the job to be known affectionately as 'Capability Cleghorn'. Of course he would never pretend to have the imagination or the ambition of old Lancelot Brown. 'Cleggers' wasn't into vast pastoral landscapes for the aristocracy. He hadn't the gear to move mountains, dig lakes, plant a forest on the skyline. But he was a grafter, and a very useful bloke to have around.

Last weekend he'd planted the first taties in Miss Angela's sheltered walled garden . . . a load of muck from Sep Robson forked in, and the King Edwards set a foot apart in the drill. Elsewhere he pruned the trees and shrubs, cut the lawns, trimmed hedges, repaired dry stone walls – and generally kept the parish in bonnie blooming order.

Tommy had lived all his life in or about Hindburn. His

47

father, old Walter Cleghorn, was a farm worker – a champion shearer in his day. Mother, born just five miles up the road, milked cows at the Glebe Farm for years . . . until she had too many bairns. They were both gone now, and the rest of the family had moved away for regular work, more pay, better houses, schools . . . whatever. But Tommy was a countryman through and through . . . a fresh air man. He had no plans to go anywhere else. He even had a plot booked in the churchyard.

Meanwhile he had another little business to supplement the gardening. A night-time job, unofficial . . . and his wife Linda and the kids often tucked in to a brace o' pheasant, a roasted rabbit, or a tasty hare for supper. They lived better than the gentry most weeks. . . .

He was working in Mrs Pollock's garden up at Haugh House . . . doing a few odd jobs, tidying up . . . when the big black car came into the drive too fast, gravel flying in all directions. He remembered thinking it looked like a gangster's car, except the windows weren't dark . . . and he could see the blokes inside weren't wearing suits and homburgs. The driver got out first and, ignoring Tommy completely, began to walk round the house looking up at the windows, into the garage, and round towards the back entrance. He was about 5ft 10in., well built, wearing trainers, jeans, denim jacket over a dirty T-shirt. He needed a shave, greasy hair. His pal, smaller, neater, sneakier, came over to where Tommy was leaning on his graip. 'Anybody in?' he asked. He lit a cigarette. Tommy thought he might be trying to act smooth, nonchalant. A real hard case. Probably a thief.

'No,' said Tommy. 'Can I help you?'

'Tarmac,' said Kev. 'Been doin' a job not far away, and there's a spare load goin' cheap. Thought y' might want the drive done. . . .'

Gazza was back from 'casing the joint' – 'So where's the boss then?' he asked.

'She's not here,' said Tommy. He didn't like the look of these two at all, and was formulating a plan of action just in case they got nasty. If push came to shove, the sneaky one might well get the graip prongs somewhere about the crotch level . . . then it would be one on one. He fancied his chances then.

'She?' asked Gazza. 'So where's the husband?'

'Business.' Tommy was trying to give nothing away. He certainly didn't buy the tarmac tale. 'They could both be back anytime now,' he said. 'Are y' gonna wait?'

'So what are you then?' The one in the denim wanted to know. 'The gardener are y'? Or the gamekeeper maybe . . .?' That seemed to amuse them.

'Why don't you bugger off,' suggested Tommy, 'and let me get on with m' work. . . .'

For a second Gazza toyed with the idea of teaching this yokel a lesson – but the graip had him worried a bit. Tommy wasn't leaning on it anymore . . . and the last thing he wanted was an 'incident'. Incidents could wait until the main event. Maybe he'd meet this cheeky sod again sometime. God help him if he ever strayed off his patch and into the Bigg Market some Saturday night. 'Huh,' was all Gazza said. It was more of a grunt. He obviously wasn't scared, and he and Kev were both giggling as they got back into the Granada.

Gazza sat behind the wheel for about ten seconds, revving the engine – then lifted his foot from the clutch. The car shot off leaving ruts in the driveway and scattering gravel onto the lawn. In fact he nearly 'lost it', and only missed the stone gate post by a whisker, as he gave a single finger salute, and howled away up the road.

'MCN 974H' – Tommy quickly scratched it onto a fag

packet with his pocket knife, before he forgot. 'Probably stolen, false number plates likely . . . but y' never know.'

Gazza stopped at a pub near the airport on their way back. Still some light in the sky. It was early, not many in. The barman preparing for the home-going office crowd. The two baddies sitting in a corner sipping ale.

'What do y' think?' asked Kev.

'What about?'

'About the job . . . do y' think it'll work?'

'Why aye,' Gazza smiled. 'They're all half asleep or away on business, or chasin' sheep. It'll be nea bother man. You just cut the wires, and we'll turn the whole village over . . . !'

'A stroll,' said Kev.

'That's right,' Gazza laughed. 'Just a stroll in the country. It's supposed to be good for y' isn't it?'

'How good?' Kev wondered.

'Hard t' tell,' said Gazza. 'Depends what Benny gives us for the antique stuff. Then there's the Post Office . . . that could be *real* money. It might add up to about ten grand a-piece . . . maybe more . . . !'

Kev raised his glass. 'Roll on Monday night,' he said.

CHAPTER SIX

Giles Pollock had three homes – a flat in Kensington, an apartment in Marbella, and Haugh House on the western edge of Hindburn. The man was a real charmer. Certainly most of the ladies thought so. He was handsome enough – with a straight, almost military bearing. His hair still thick and dark at fifty-something. A nose that might have been ever so slightly rearranged, perhaps on a rugby field, or maybe by a cuckolded husband. Only he knew. No one ever saw him other than immaculate. On business trips he wore one of a dozen dark woollen suits, generally a pale blue striped shirt and a perfectly knotted silk CBI tie. A briefcase with coded lock, and the initials GHP, would be tossed onto the rear seat of his white 500 SL, along with a brown Abercrombie overcoat, a folded brolly . . . and off he'd go, showered and cologned, to astonish the business world. It would have astonished Giles to learn that a lad from the Primrose estate in Newcastle already had his eye on the Merc . . . even had a buyer lined up in Bradford.

But it hadn't all been plain sailing for Mr Pollock. After the Applepeel affair, not all his ducks had been competent swimmers. Somewhat bored after the intoxication of growth and float, he had taken over one or two small troubled companies, convinced his acumen, his genius, would revive them. But it hadn't always worked. Too often they had been involved in fields he really knew little or nothing about. His arrogant self-confidence, the naive and dangerous conviction that *he* could make money anywhere, anytime, where others had failed – proved ill-founded. One large manufacturing outfit, bought from the receivers, lasted less than a year. Another he was lucky to sell to a management buy-out for half his original investment.

His self-belief may have faltered occasionally, but it was seldom apparent. Always the gregarious social animal, he continued to beguile the wives and amuse the husbands with tales of high finance, and a fund of risqué stories. What's more he always remembered names. The briefest of introductions – and months later he could instantly draw from his magical memory bank. 'Hallo, wonderful to see you again . . . Victoria isn't it? How *are* you?' And of course Victoria would be immensely flattered, hanging on his every compliment – convinced she'd never been out of his thoughts since last they met. Oh yes, he could certainly talk. A good voice too – even through smoke, alcohol and the party hubbub, he had a deep clear tone that never showed the strain . . . didn't need to force its way into a noisy conversation. He would stand there in the centre of a room, a little taller than most, easily, attractively, holding court.

Many of the Hindburn locals couldn't stand 'the smarmy bugger'. . . . Reckoned he'd get his comeuppance sooner or later. Geordie Dodds thought he probably 'couldn't lie straight in bed'.

However, in spite of a few setbacks, and a questionable reputation, the man was suddenly in the big league again. When the board of Euroform decided they could benefit from his contacts, his linguistic talents, his marketing expertise, Giles quickly ditched all other interests, and dived eagerly into the muddy waters of the EEC. That was three years ago.

They gave him a title: 'Executive Contract Manager'. Provided offices, staff and apartments in London, Brussels and Rome. His remit to implement whatever complicated business schemes were conceived by the directors of the group. To the best of his knowledge, he never met any of these people. They remained shadowy and anonymous figures . . . a voice on the phone, a message on a fax. Indeed there was virtually none of the normal business fraternisation within the company. Nobody, it seemed, knew the *whole* murky structure, and yet somewhere in this organisation there was definitely an inner circle, a star chamber, solely concerned with using and benefiting from the convoluted machine that drove the Common Market. And as far as he could tell, they seldom missed a trick.

In the beginning he was somewhat unnerved by the very scale of the operation, profits like intercontinental telephone numbers. Politicians and bureaucrats, harbour masters and transport managers, clerks and wagon drivers, all tempted and bribed into a vast web of intrigue. It took him about eighteen months to realise the enormous potential sloshing about in there – and the opportunities to play at least some of this 'game' to his own advantage. As he became more and more familiar with the system, and especially after he met his friend Arturo in Milan, Giles Pollock's greed grew and grew, and finally got the better of him. A little cream off the top? Who would miss it? Arturo and others were at it already. A mere one per cent of a contract syphoned off, moved, shuffled into some remote account? Who would find it? Backhanders and greased palms – everybody was doing it. Indeed the whole ridiculous scheme of things demanded it. Avarice inspired it! He'd read somewhere of six billion pounds 'stolen' from the CAP, every year – and inexorably his snout dipped deeper and deeper into the trough.

He came home to his country house on the edge of the village about once a month. It was a refuge. A place to breathe deeply, recharge the cells for the next foray into 'wonderland'. He realised it couldn't go on forever, of course not. . . . This was fraud, it was larceny on a grand scale. Perhaps one could argue that robbing from the great EEC 'elephant' was fair game. But Giles was now into a much riskier business altogether . . . he was actually stealing from his fellow thieves. Double jeopardy. They wouldn't be very impressed with that, if they ever found out . . . and of course they *would*, sooner or later. He knew it.

In fact, he'd already decided to give it no more than another couple of months before he called it a day. He had over two million hidden away already. South Africa looked attractive. He wouldn't be taking Polly, however. Marianne from the finance department in Luxembourg would be a more suitable companion, he reckoned . . . shrewd, classy, sassy. She liked money too.

Meanwhile relax, play the country gent . . . have a few people in for drinks, drop into the pub, chat with the locals. No business this weekend, except perhaps the odd fax to our man in Rome . . . book a flight for Tuesday, that's all. Take it easy.

The Sunday morning before the robbery dawned damp, dull and still. After a late breakfast, he set off on foot to collect the papers. A walk would do him good. Spring in the air . . . just. Polly's daffodils along the driveway reaching up out of the grass . . . snowdrops, past their best now, still peeping out from under the hedge . . . sparrows and chaffinches gossiping there. Up beside Hindhope a red tractor with a yellow fertiliser spinner on the back, going up and down a hill side, even paced, straight lines, giving some crop its nitrogen boost. Turn left down the lonnen, and looking over towards Clartiehole, even Giles, a city boy, could see the countryside was 'greening up'. Ewes and lambs in the fields now. He leaned on a gate for a while watching the sheep – the mothers mostly grazing, young ones playing games. It was a pleasant picture. The landscape looked neat and tidy, well ordered. He saw Sep a long way off leaning on his stick, watching, checking the animals . . . dog at heel, waiting – looking up at his master. Giles waved, but either Sep didn't see him, or maybe he was more concerned with other things.

At the bottom of the hill he turned left again, back towards the village – and there was Geordie Dodds coming out of his shed carrying a pair of lambs . . . a ewe fussing and anxious, following behind. Twenty yards into the field he put his load down, gave them a nudge with a wellie and left the family to themselves. Geordie looked up, nodded to Giles, and disappeared back inside.

The little Post Office was busy. The usual Sunday morning gathering in search of royal scandal, political ineptitude, premier league results, true life confessions and a tin of peaches for lunch. He picked up *The Sunday Times*, a packet of small cigars, smiled his dazzling 'Good morning' at everyone who looked his way, and sauntered over to the pub. A gin 'n' tonic seemed a very good idea.

Twelve noon and the Hart was filling up. A few retired couples out for the day, considering the bar menu. Some locals he recognised, enjoying their ritual Sunday morning pint, comparing rural notes, swapping gossip . . . and (inevitably) discussing the weather again. 'Bad forecast,' said somebody. . . . 'It'll be right enough – with the wind in that art y' canna expect anythin' else. . . . It's not settled.' Giles took his drink to a quiet seat, and opened his paper at the Business section, one eye on his portfolio . . . one ear on the chatter.

At the far end of the bar a group of farmers were contrasting their lambing disasters . . . trying to outdo each other with tragic tales of sheep, determined to die.

'We had this yow wi' twin lamb disease yesterday,' said one of them. 'So I says to Michael, I says come wi' me and I'll show y' a bloody miracle. She was lyin' in the stackyard lookin' awful sorry for herself . . . y' know what they're like. But I thinks to m'self, not t' worry – a bottle of glucose into the bitch, and she'll be up 'n' away. You'll have done it yourselves many a day. It's dramatic isn't it? Works a treat every time . . . and I says t' m'self, I says – young Michael's never seen it done before . . . he'll think I'm a genius! So anyway, I shoved in the needle, holds the bottle up high, and lets the stuff run straight in, nea bother. . . .'

They were listening with smiles on their faces. Some of them knew what was coming.

'You'll not believe it,' the man went on, 'but the rotten sod leapt up, staggered about five yards . . . and dropped stone dead! I was absolutely foamin' . . . I kept pokin' her with m' stick, sure she'd blink and stand up . . . . but the bugger never moved . . . never moved! – And I tell y' what . . . Michael wasn't very impressed either . . . laughed like a drain!'

They all chuckled and drank their beer, Giles half watching, half listening. 'We had a suicide last week,' said a long lean shepherd, all hands and feet, and a boney red face . . .

'This four crop mule wi' twins went and hanged herself. Don't ask me how, but there she was the other mornin', with her head fast under the lid of the hayheck. I mean she must've nudged it open somehow, stuffed her muckle greedy head inside, and got thoroughly stuck when it blew shut again. . . . Anyway, she was . . . choked or hanged, it doesn't matter . . . dead as a crow, danglin' with her back feet just barely touchin' the ground. . . .' He was coming to the punch-line. 'And would y' credit it,' he said, 'there were her two lambs, still suckin' away on the corpse like good 'n's . . . determined to get the very last drop! . . . wouldn't let go!'

Geordie Dodds and Tommy Thompson came in, laughing about something else. A quick pint – no more than one mind you, or Geordie would want to sleep all afternoon, and that would never do. He'd left Amanda in charge for an hour. She was chuffed to bits.

There were five or six farmery folk at the bar now, an exclusive untidy little group detached from the smarter passing trade. Giles heard snippets of their banter as it flitted from sheep to weather to the price of beef. There was talk of ewe quotas, set-aside, cereal acreage payments and how the crops were looking. Some chat about a pair of townie thieves in the neighbourhood . . . up to no good. Tales of bureaucratic intrusion and political incompetence. Just a bunch of farmers complaining as usual. Nothing fresh. Giles wasn't all that interested.

'Records and documents for everything now,' growled a man with an oily cap stuck on the back of his bald head. 'Fell a rotten tree, bury a dead yow . . . you have to write it all down. I'm never out of the damned office . . . canna get any proper work done.' He drained his glass and pushed it over for a refill. 'It's all gettin' far too complicated for the likes o' me,' he said sadly. 'Same again Jack.'

A weather-beaten bloke leaning on the counter, grinning. 'Heard a good 'n' yesterday,' he said. 'Y' know Alfie Sanderson at the South Steads – well he's apparently into all this newfangled technical gear now . . . computer, fax machine, mobile phone – the lot. Carries his pocket telephone wherever he goes. Thinks he's a tycoon! Anyway he was sittin' in the tractor ploughin' one day last week, when a rep comes into the field t' bid him for some barley . . . Alfie, sharp as a needle, thinks he'll just check the prices, phone around, get a few more quotes, impress this bloke. So out comes the fancy phone, and he's sittin' there in the cab punchin' numbers and blatherin' t' every merchant in the county. . . . No end of a swell. After about twenty minutes he sends the rep packin', says he'll think about it . . . and drives away up the field. It was tea time before he realised he'd left the phone lyin' on the tractor mudguard – and it must've fallen off. He's ploughed the bloody thing in, hasn't he. Lost!'

They were all chuckling at the story, but the man wasn't quite finished. 'Alfie's wife finds him at the darkenin', crawlin' up and down the field with his ear to the furrow – waitin' for somebody to ring 'im . . .!!'

Giles stood up and took his empty glass back to the bar. Time to go . . . a few letters to write. Lunch would be in the oven. He should've just tossed a passing greeting to the little gathering standing there, but he couldn't resist a parting shot. These peasants always protested too much. Didn't they realise they'd never had it so good. This was a golden era for agriculture . . . wasn't it?

'Discussing where to invest your newfound wealth?' he asked with his usual charming smile. 'I bet there aren't many Euro-sceptics here, eh?'

For a few seconds they only stared at him. They knew who he was right enough, where he lived, what sort of car he drove. They weren't too sure what he did these days, often away on business. Probably dodgy. Seriously rich . . . a bit too clever . . . canny wife though. . . .

The man who had performed the 'miracle' operation on the late ewe eventually said, 'What y' mean?' And perhaps Giles had the chance to back off . . . 'Just joking, have a nice day . . . hope the weather improves for you lads,' . . . something like that would've done. But he didn't. In another world, in another bar, in another company, he would have more than held his own, made a mark, won the argument . . . closed the deal. He should have known this was not his pond.

'Oh c'mon,' Giles grinned, 'I know all about EEC subsidies. Good God you're even paid to grow nothing . . . twenty quid a head for your breeding sheep . . . sell your mad cow quota and retire. It's easy!'

Geordie Dodds was briefly tempted to hit him. He'd had a bad enough night in the lambing shed, without this loud-mouthed character telling him how easy it was. He could have told him he thought the whole CAP pantomime was an expensive bloody farce . . . that set-aside was a nonsense . . . how politicians, and lawyers, and fat cats like Pollock were giving democracy a bad name . . . but he didn't.

Instead he said simply, 'Aye well, I can tell y' there's still some bits of farmin' that haven't changed very much, and if I don't get back t' those animals, I'll be payin' for it likely. . . . See y' lads. . . .' And with that he picked up his stick and left.

So did the rest of them. They downed the last dregs of ale in the bottom of their glasses, and went home . . . without a word . . . just a nod to the barman.

Giles followed them out into the car park, slightly bewildered. Largely ignored, but apparently undismayed, he tucked the newspaper under his arm and strode up the village towards his roast beef and Yorkshire pudding . . . and a glass or two of Burgundy. Past the little shop, closed now . . . past the garage with its three sleeping pumps . . . past the Dawson cottage with its 'For Sale' sign in the garden. £120,000 they wanted for it. He'd overheard some prattle in the Post Office earlier. They'd been here less than a year, but Mrs D. simply couldn't stand the 'quiet'. Nobody to talk to, she said. No decent shops within miles. Restaurants, theatre, chemist, they all required a trip in the car. She'd never settled. It hadn't been at all as she'd expected, but then maybe she was never really clear what she expected in the first place. Rather woolly images of friendly country women, making chutney perhaps. Big handsome red-faced men with horses . . . Constable scenes, the sun shining, nice smells. . . .

And what did she find? Certainly no chutney ladies. Not much chat either, it seems. Lonely. Most villagers commuted back into the city every day, and left her sitting there, drinking tea and knitting, and watching afternoon TV. Summer wasn't so bad, but the winter had been quite awful. So much snow! Hindburn had been blocked in for three days – no lights, central heating off, no cooker, no electric blanket! God, it was like the middle ages. The quicker they got back to civilisation the better. Mr Dawson wouldn't argue, he usually did as he was told – no option. Another winter out in the sticks would probably kill them both anyway!

It was this thought of options that stuck in Giles's mind. Indeed he might even be obliged to make *his* move pretty soon . . . before the options disappeared altogether. He would definitely have to stay one step ahead, or he was done for. The 'Management' wouldn't just slap his wrist. He had to go *before* they suspected anything. Maybe he'd had his hand in the honey jar long enough. . . . By the time he got home, Giles had made a decision to quit next week.

'Somebody trying to get you on the phone,' Polly shouted from the kitchen. 'A woman, foreign accent . . . said she'd try later. . . .' She couldn't care less who it was. Some French bit he had on the side probably . . . so what? She was more concerned about the Yorkshire puddings. They seemed reluctant to rise. . . .

Giles opened a bottle of wine left warming by the radiator, poured himself a glass and took the bottle into his office. He'd ring Marianne back later, when Polly was out for a walk. Maybe call Arturo as well. He just had a sneaking feeling that something unexpected was about to happen. . . . It made him feel distinctly uneasy.

CHAPTER SEVEN

On the preceding Thursday afternoon, in broad daylight, Kevin nicked a white Ford transit from down by the Quayside. He was lucky. He'd watched it for over an hour as it made deliveries to pubs and restaurants. 'Smithson's Catering Services' stencilled on both sides, a cartoon chef with a big friendly grin painted on the back doors. M reg. Just the job.

A fat bloke in a white coat, who looked as if he might occasionally help himself to selections from his load, carried a tray of goodies into the Baltic Inn. He left the sliding driver's door open, but took the keys with him. Kev sauntered past, looking into the cab as he paused and lit a cigarette. It wouldn't be too difficult for a man of his talents, but he'd need a few seconds to get it going.

Fattie came back too soon, whistling some tuneless dirge. A clipboard in one hand and the keys in the other. He drove a hundred yards along the street, and stopped opposite a coffee bar. Same procedure. Round to the back of the van, opened the double doors with the ignition key, took out a large cardboard box of stotties or whatever, banged the doors shut with his right foot, locked up, and crossed the street into the café. Kevin watched him through the window, pretending to look at a menu displayed there . . . hoping the man might sit down, have a chat, drink a cappuccino. But no such luck – he just dumped the package, got a signature on the delivery note, and was on his way out in no time at all.

This performance was repeated at a further three stops, and Kev, who had trailed the vehicle on foot along the crowded pavement, had almost given up on this one when fate intervened, in the shape of a smart BMW.

The transit had doubled back under the Tyne Bridge, negotiated the busy roundabout at the bottom of The Side, and was obviously heading for one of the eating places below Castle Stairs. Kev was watching him, but had more or less decided to abandon the project, and go for a pint – when the car pulled out of a parking space somewhere near the Guildhall . . . and gently 'dunched' the van. Nothing very serious. Probably a sales rep who'd enjoyed a long business lunch . . . maybe one more glass of wine than he'd really intended. Congratulating himself on a good deal, not concentrating, obviously didn't look in the mirror. Careless, that's all.

But it stopped the traffic. The well-dressed business chappie got out to stare in dismay at the bent offside wing of his pride and joy. Fatso went bananas. He jammed on the brakes and leapt out onto the street, obviously very disappointed at this turn of events. He simply ignored all the other vehicles, waved his fist and pointed dramatically at the graze along the side of his van. The sales person appeared to be in a trance, as Fatso screamed into his face.

'What the hell were y' playin' at . . .? You never looked, you didn't indicate. It's your bloody fault, y' realise that don't y'? I want your name and address and insurance company before y' bugger off . . .!'

He turned to fetch pen and paper from the cab — just in time to see the grinning cartoon chef on the back doors accelerate into the traffic, and disappear beyond the Copthorne Hotel. Gone.

Kev turned right up Forth Banks, across Scotswood Road, up Blenheim Street onto Westgate. Left into the maze of Elswick . . . and the transit was behind locked doors in the Benwell garage within fifteen minutes of the 'steal'.

It wouldn't need much doing to it . . . a common enough motor, hundreds just like it. Change the plates, of course, remove Smithson's name and the chef logo. Give it a complete new personality before morning. Easy.

* * *

The following day, Wally the weasel was at the Victoria Jubilee Infirmary in North Shields, when he rang Gazza from reception. He'd gone there on the bus with his mother and her varicose veins, for a ten o'clock appointment. They were still sitting there at one-thirty. He'd read all the women's magazines, drunk about a gallon of tea, eaten three KitKats . . . and now they were taking her to X-ray. God what a drag. . . . It seemed everybody in Shields had a ten o'clock appointment that day. The waiting areas were crowded with coughing, wheezing, spluttering, limping, bandaged listless victims. There were wheelchairs and beds parked in corridors, people shuffling along on crutches, sticks and zimmer frames, while the staff scurried back and forth carrying volumes of case notes. Doctors were dealing with tumours and toenails, cancer and constipation with the same strained equanimity. And there was no smoking!

Wally couldn't take much more of this. He'd gone into the car park for a fag. In fact he smoked three, one after the other, as he wandered aimlessly through the rows of vehicles in the cool sunshine. Thinking about this and that, as people do. He thought about his mother. Big fat Bella, poor auld woman – she'd had a rough time. Six bairns to bring up, none of them much use really. Wayne serving in the army somewhere, not a word from him in two years. Dawn serving pizzas in Jarrow. Gavin serving time in gaol – where Wally was last year. Scott and Darren were still at school . . . or at least some days they were – and already into petty thievin', nea chance. Father? . . . long gone, last seen on a ship with a foreign name sailin' down the Tyne, bound for God knows where . . . Wally didn't miss him at all. He was always drunk anyway, and knocked Bella about most nights after he'd had a 'skinful'. Good riddance.

And now here she was at the Jubilee, her fat lumpy legs hurtin' like hell . . . and waiting, waiting, waiting for somebody to give her relief on the National Health.

The family lived at the bottom end of Hope Street, No. 76. Now there was a sick joke, if ever there was one. Not much bloody hope as far as Wally could see. The houses were a damp disgrace . . . the street littered with rubbish and dog crap. No gardens, no trees. If he couldn't get out with Gazza and the lads now and then, earn a quid or two on the side t' supplement the 'dole' – he'd go crackers.

Funny, he was just thinking about Gazza and the next big job, when he saw the van. Well, just the top of it really – about five rows away, dark blue, skylight in the roof. A little closer and he could see it was exactly what Gazza said they needed. Good nick, carry a ton . . . J reg.

He ran all the way back to main reception, and looked for the public phones. They were all engaged of course, except the one on the end, but it was out of order. He waited ages for somebody to hang up. 'That's all you ever do in hospitals isn't it?' he thought. 'Wait, wait, wait . . . hurry up and wait again.' He debated whether to risk a ten or a fifty on the call, looked at the ceiling for a while, struggled to remember the number, and finally got through to the Strawberry. That's where he'd be at this hour, definitely.

'Can y' take it?' asked Gazza when they found him.

'If it's still there,' said Wally, 'I think so.'

'Do it,' said Gazza. 'You know where to go.'

Wally attracted no attention as he hurried back along the corridors and out into the car park again. Everybody in the whole world was at the hospital today, he was just another visitor going for a smoke probably. There were about twenty nicotine addicts under the porch at the side exit puffing away, two of them nurses. Outside, the day had taken a turn for the worse . . . dull now, cloudy . . . beginning to drizzle. 'Champion,' Wally thought. It meant people wouldn't be hanging about.

The vehicle was still there, nobody anywhere near. He might have to break a window, but no matter. He wasn't carrying any tools today, didn't think he'd need them. A brick, picked up from a little extension job near 'Cardiac Thoracic', wrapped in his anorak smashed the passenger side glass at the second attempt. He chose that window for three reasons. One, it was next to the wall of the hospital generator building . . . no other vehicle on that side. Two, he didn't want glass sticking up his arse on the driver's seat, and three, if somebody appeared while he was wiring the ignition, they'd come to the driver's door, wouldn't they? That would be locked with the window up, and Wally would slip out the other side and scarper. . . .

If anyone had been timing him, the clock would've stopped at forty-five seconds from entry to ignition. He reversed carefully out of the line, looked both ways, fastened the belt, wound the broken window out of sight, and drove sedately out into Hawkey's Lane. He turned right, then left on Trevor Terrace, and set off for Wallsend and the city. There was nobody running after him.

The VW's tank was about quarter full, so that was okay. The radio worked. He found Atlantic 252 and Mariah Carey, lit another cigarette and relaxed.

Wally crossed the central motorway at half-past three, drove west up Gallowgate onto Stanhope Street and peeped the horn outside the Benwell 'lock-up' ten minutes later. They were expecting him, Gazza had already been on the phone.

It wasn't until he was on the bus heading back to the Haymarket that he remembered his mother.

* * *

Sol got the gun on Friday night. Friday was a good night to do this sort of business. The city was busy. The weekend started here. Revellers and ravers everywhere, in and out of the pubs and clubs, way into Saturday morning. It was easy to 'operate' unnoticed in the crowd. So many bodies milling about, in the Bigg Market, on the Quayside, up by the Monument – the law could never hope to cope with every little drunken disturbance. They kept a low profile. Meanwhile drink, drugs, sex, violence – whatever turned you on – it was all there, 'doon the toon'. A 'pot pourri' of grass, skunk, E, speed, coke . . . whatever, readily available . . . if you knew where to look, who to ask . . . and had the money. A kind of jungle culture set to techno music, filled with primitive power struggles, rites and rituals. . . . A threat of danger just below the revelry, sometimes bubbling into a punch-up, that kept most of the natives in line, and frightened off strangers. It was all about 'territory'. At a personal level, you found a place, a space – surrounded yourself with mates and just went with the flow, had a good time. On a higher more menacing plane was the 'business' territory, the drug money territory. Only two or three teams played *that* game . . . and you didn't play on someone else's pitch.

Sol was on door duty from nine to midnight, half an hour's break inside . . . then back on the step until Joanna's closed about 3.00 am, or whenever the gaffer decided. The early shift was seldom any trouble. A queue of punters would form out in the cold. Good natured banter, competitive mating games, 'pick-ups' and put-downs, slowly moving towards Sol and his partner, and the beat beyond. To the big lads in the dark dinner jackets and dark glasses. The 'heavies' with the power. Sometimes they kept the line waiting, not because the club was full, far from it . . . but simply to increase the size of the queue, and give an impression that *this* was the only place to be tonight. Everybody wanted to be in there . . . look at them! The regular clubbers creeping towards the pleasure dome. At last inside, past the massive 'chest in yer face', and up the steps – into the dim seduction of the foyer, through 'membership', and beyond . . . to the disco music, the strobic lights, the sweaty dancing, the drink, the chat-up, the dope. The beginning of Friday night live! There was a dress code of sorts, especially to get in, but the girls got away with almost anything . . . or almost nothing. Even after a year in this job, Sol was still transfixed, goggle-eyed, open-mouthed, by the long lean lasses (some of them real beauties) who smiled as they passed, and left little to his limited imagination. He could 'score' every night if he wanted. Or at least that's what he told the lads.

'So what y' want a gun for?' Victor asked. 'Are y' gonna rob Barclays or somewhere?' They were in the back office just after midnight. Sol only grinned and shrugged his enormous shoulders. His head almost disappeared when he did that. 'Just for a frightener,' he said, 'We'll likely never use it.'

Victor wasn't convinced. 'Aye, that's what they all say ... then y' get yourself into an awkward situation, and y' have to blast your way out. Y' say sorry I was just pretendin' ... didn't *mean* to shoot you. ...' He was teasing – sitting there behind his big mahogany desk, photographs of famous clients who'd been in here hanging around the walls ... footballers, pop stars, a couple of boxers. The lighting was subdued, and half a dozen TV screens relayed instant images from every corner of the club. Harry, the ever-ready hard man sitting in the corner. This inner sanctum almost sound-proof. Nobody got in here without a thorough investigation ... and not everyone got out in exactly the same condition they went in.

'So what you need?' Victor asked. 'Hand piece, shotgun – what?'

Sol was playing with the ring in his ear, never comfortable in this room, out of his depth. 'Gazza says a short four-ten would be good,' he said quietly ... 'or a twelve bore. ... He'll pay, naturally.'

'Naturally,' said Victor, and stood up from the desk. A short thick-set man, all-year tan, not much hair left, smart suit ... fifty-ish. He came round and stood in front of Sol. 'Tell y' what,' he said. 'I don't like giving dangerous toys to little boys ... because if anything goes wrong, they *might* tell somebody where they got it. ...' Victor didn't blink until he was sure the message had got through. 'However,' he went on, 'seeing as how y' work for me, and you're a canny lad ... we'll make an exception. I'll fix it for you, or at least Harry here will. See him before you leave.'

That was it. Sol's nervous little interview was over. Back to his post on the door. No mention of money, or when,

69

how, or where. Maybe it was a favour . . . a favour to be repaid somehow at a later date, of course. Victor always had a few favours outstanding. There was even a list somewhere – and most of the names on it were far more influential than young Sol. This was small beer.

The only bit of bother the bouncing brigade had that night was with a drunken scrap dealer from County Durham. Supported by a bimbo under each arm, he seemed determined to show everyone just what a terror he was. Loud, aggressive, pushing and shoving as he made his way to the door. The girls shrieking at his foul language, as if he were the wittiest man in town. But it took him too long to leave. He was upsetting other customers . . . bumping and very boring. He would probably be sick at any moment, and Sol moved to escort him to the line of black taxis waiting outside . . . get him off the premises with as little fuss as possible.

Scrap-man was not to be hustled, though. He'd spent a fortune priming these two tarts with very expensive Asti Spumante, and no gorilla was going to lead him out onto the street by the nose. Unwisely, he took a swing at the gorilla, and said something very impolite about his mother. It was an error he was to reflect upon, when he recovered consciousness an hour later, just off Dean Street. He would also be disappointed to find the bimbos were long gone – as was his wallet, credit cards and car keys. Fortunately, he still had a handkerchief with which to wipe his bloody bent nose.

At the end of business Harry always ran some of the staff home in the Trooper. It was part of the service. In the wee small hours, he would deliver them to various points throughout the city, and (almost) see them safely into their cold dark beds. Tonight, Sol was the last 'drop', and just as he opened the front door, Harry produced a parcel from under one of the passenger seats. It was a roll of threadbare stair carpet, about three feet from end to end. Inside something wrapped in hessian. They both knew what it was, so they didn't say anything. Just, 'So long, see y' ' . . . and the Trooper was away.

*   *   *

Saturday afternoon in the Strawberry, Gazza, Wally, Kev and Sol met for a couple of jars before the match.

'We're ready,' said Gazza. 'A little paint job on the transit, and that's it.' The friend at the Benwell lock-up would fix a roof rack with sliding ladders . . . put a different logo on the sides. The gun with four cartridges was under the floorboards somewhere on the Primrose estate, together with overalls and assorted tools.

'Right then – we'll meet Monday night at Armstrong Street . . . ten o'clock sharp. Nobody be late,' said Gazza. 'And no bloody booze at dinner time, okay? We'll go to Hindburn a bit early – have a look round before midnight . . . just to make sure there's no nasty surprises . . . right?'

United beat West Ham two nowt . . . Ferdinand and Ginola. Gazza said it was a good sign. Not long now.

CHAPTER EIGHT

Geordie Dodds's notion that he might be the only villager not a-bed on that damp Monday night was far from accurate. For a start Gloria was wide awake. Sweet scented, and seductively framed in the doorway that led from lounge to bedroom. She was carrying a bottle of Glenfiddich and two glasses, and had 'carelessly' left the light on behind her, and as she was now dressed in nothing more than a diaphanous negligee, the silhouette was having quite a disturbing effect on her guest.

'You're not in a hurry are you?' she smiled.

James had appeared about eight o'clock – lost, or so he said, asking the way to Edinburgh. His car pulled up outside the cottage five minutes after she arrived home from work, and a drink with the girls from the office. She just had time to put some heating on and boil the kettle, before he knocked on her door. He drove a hired Mondeo, Lynx aftershave she thought, smart, well dressed. Just the faintest hint of a foreign accent – quite sexy . . . and could he use her phone? His mobile miracle wouldn't function here for some reason.

'Hindburn's in a bit of a hole,' Gloria explained, 'surrounded by hills . . . those things seldom work properly down in the village – you've got to drive up beyond Hindhope, to the top of the bank. Maybe that's what they mean by high-tech. . . .' she grinned.

He'd come in, dialled a number, and talked briefly to somebody somewhere about a delivery early tomorrow, left a pound coin by the phone, and settled himself on the sofa with a cup of coffee. He had watched Gloria like a predatory ferret as she glided about the house, settling in for the night, changing out of her smart 'office' suit, and eventually dissolving into an easy chair no more than an arm's length away. James felt no real urgency to move on, not yet anyway. This spot would do nicely. That was two hours and half a bottle of whisky ago. Things had progressed quite well since then. Now he moved purposefully towards the tempting vision in the doorway, unbuttoning his shirt as he went. Gloria turning slowly, looking over her shoulder, as her guest followed the hips towards the bedroom.

* * *

Sep Robson at Clartiehole Farm was wide awake as well, though his companion at this time was hardly being so co-operative. In fact she was dying!

Sep had ministered to her every need for days . . . showered her with all the miracles of modern medicine, spoken encouragingly, reminded the old girl of her family responsibilities, even threatened her with a much quicker death, if she didn't buck up her ideas . . . but the geriatric 'udders only' mule was determined to go. And she had two canny lambs as well. The second death in a week. Bugger it!

He picked up the twins, one tucked under his arm, the other carried by the front legs, and made his way to the old stable. He dropped the poor wee orphans into the 'pet pen', to join two others already there. Straw bales all around them, a lamp overhead to warm the cold motherless nights. Somebody would have to give them a drink before too long – what a bloody nuisance. Gladys would look after them come morning, but it might be unfair to wake her now. . . . In any case Willie would be taking over in a few minutes. He did the night shift, eleven to seven.

Five minutes early, son of Sep stumbled into the lambing shed, well wrapped up against the chill draught, rubbing his hands, flapping arms, stamping feet. He'd been watching highlights of a boring football match – nowts-a-piece after extra time – and although it was cosy enough in front of the telly, he wasn't too dismayed at the prospect of relieving the auld man. Somebody had to do it. Y' certainly couldn't leave the yowes to their own devices, not all night. It would be chaos by the morning.

Sep gave Willie his up-to-the-minute report on the evening's developments. He pointed out a couple of sheep likely to produce before dawn, mentioned the new orphans over in the stable, and a set of triplets born within the last hour. They might end up as a pair, one lamb wasn't very strong . . . keep an eye on 'im . . . and get rid of this dead body. See y' in the mornin'.

In the cosy kitchen he made himself a cup of cocoa, found some digestive biscuits, and began to undress by the Aga. There was quite a lot to come off, but it took no time at all. The wellies were already discarded at the back door. Socks, overalls and trousers were removed as one, as was vest, shirt and two pullovers – all into another heap . . . and before you could say 'Goodnight sweetheart,' Sep was creeping in beside big warm comfortable Gladys. It took his ever-lovin' wife about five slow seconds to realise that the cosy snugly world, which until now she had been happily occupying alone, was being cruelly invaded by some awful bloodless creature from outer space, with feet like dead haddock, and a massive freezing paw, that even now was groping about under her nightie, in search of a bosom.

She squealed, kicked out backwards, shuffled over . . . but quickly went back to sleep. Gladys was not a woman easily disturbed.

*   *   *

Gordon Graham, at the vicarage, was awake too. There was a mouse in his right hand. He was staring at a blank computer screen . . . not concentrating. It didn't take much to disturb *him* these nights. Those bleating sheep just across the road at the Glebe Farm for a start! There always seemed to be some pathetic wailing animal wandering about in the middle of the night. That miserable plaintive cry of a lost lamb who didn't care what time it was. Mr Dodds kept hens too, and the cockerel crowed, not just at dawn as he'd been led to believe in coloured story books – but at any time day or night . . . whenever fancy took the mad sex-crazed fool. Why didn't somebody barbecue the bastard??

And the bells. The dull cracked stroke of every hour from St Mary's Church tower only a few yards beyond his garden wall. He desperately tried to get to sleep soon after midnight, in the hope that somehow, one, two and three o'clock might not be enough to wake him . . . but he often found himself lying waiting (still desperate) for the knell that summoned him alert again.

There was no doubt about it, this whole rural adventure had been an unmitigated disaster. Peace? Tranquillity? A cleaner, slower more meaningful way of life??? Nothing but nonsense! There were tractors roaring through the village almost every day. At harvest time, monster combines shuffled from farm to farm, like flightless Jumbos, revving round the War Memorial. Endless trailer loads of grain were ferried to the drier down near the A1. Then came the straw convoys. Big round shiny yellow bales piled three high on giant wagons, heading west into the hills for weeks on end. Some of them never made it. One weekend last September there were at least four enormous bales left lying at the crossroads, two on the verge by Foggin's garage, several more at the bridge over the Marleyburn, and a couple near the village hall. In fact the road was virtually blocked, until Donald Peabody at Paddock House (never one to ignore an unsolicited bonus) somehow managed to roll them out of sight with a friend's Shogun – and fed them to his little potbellied animals. They thought it was Christmas.

And all these farm machines were gigantic now. You simply couldn't get past the damned things on a country road. Only yesterday, late for the office, Gordon had been stuck behind a tractor with double wheels, and a huge hunk of cultivating equipment attached. At least that's what he assumed it was, he wasn't really sure. He knew it was certainly agricultural, it was very big, and it had a half-mile queue of raging commuters in powerful motorcars stuck behind it. The tractor driver, in a soundproof air conditioned cab, was apparently oblivious to all this, and probably listening to 'Five Live'. He never looked back until he turned into a ploughed field near Molesdon, and then waved everybody on with a bright bucolic grin. The bloody cheek!

And those animals . . . disgusting beasts, dung every-where. His wife Shelagh (a physiotherapist at the General), who'd seen many a disturbing sight in the course of her career, actually came upon two cattle fornicating in broad daylight. They were right there in the churchyard, of all places. She had been appalled, naturally – and assuming one must be a bull, and consequently very dangerous, had immediately phoned Mr Dodds to retrieve his violent and shameless creatures.

'We haven't got a bull,' said Geordie. 'But a couple o' heifers were in heat last night, and they're missin' this mornin'. . . . That'll be them likely – daft buggers!'

Poor Mrs Graham had been quite shaken for the rest of the week. 'You'll never believe what we have to put up with in this village,' she told her mother on the phone. 'The noise, the smells, the traffic . . . and now lesbian cows everywhere!'

'For God's sake come home,' cried mother, 'if only for the sake of the children.'

* * *

At the new exclusive executive houses up at Hindhope Farm *everybody* was awake. Sep had forgotten to turn off the 'banger' again, and it was firing an anti-pigeon salvo at irregular intervals across a field of oilseed rape, somewhere beyond the trees, just over the road.

Hindhope had been one of those traditional old farming outposts that fell victim to the rural economic tide in the late eighties. Antiquated byres and stables, once mucked out by hand, transformed into desirable country homes . . . each with a paddock for the obligatory pony. The land split up and sold off to surrounding farmers. Hindhope Farm a farm no more. A sign of the times.

Sep and Willie Robson at Clartiehole had acquired the fields south of the road. It fitted in nicely with what they had already, and pushed Clartiehole up to over four hundred acres . . . a much more 'viable' unit. . . . It might support the family for another generation or two.

Freddie Fox QC at what was now known as No. 2 Hindhope Court could stand the bombardment no longer, and angrily dialled the Clartiehole number at about midnight. He had a hurriedly prepared catalogue of dire legal threats to deliver, even at this hour.

Sep heard the phone ringing alright, but he was warm now – Gladys was settled again. He was damned if he was getting out of bed. Instead, he sank even lower under the blankets, and waited for the caller to lose patience. It took a while.

A bleary-eyed Barry Beeday, the plumber in No. 3, had tried to phone Foxie while the line was still engaged. Joe Gaskett, second-hand car dealer in No. 1, had even wandered, half naked, out into the yard, and met Gerald the stockbroker from the old farmhouse, standing in his dressing gown, shining a torch in the general direction of the 'artillery'.

'Do you think it's a poacher?' asked Gaskett, feeling the cold damp air creeping up his nightshirt.

'I know exactly what it is,' said Gerald. 'It's one of those gas-fired bird scarer things . . . and if I knew how to turn the bloody thing off . . . Foxie should sue that old bugger Robson for public nuisance, disturbing the peace, noise pollution . . . anything!'

When they saw everybody's lights were on, all four men ended up in various styles of night attire in Foxie's kitchen, plotting the downfall of Sep, and every other heartless inconsiderate peasant for miles around.

'Did you get a whiff of that stuff he was spreading on the west field last week,' somebody said. 'Absolutely disgusting. We could smell it in the house for days!'

'Came out of church on Sunday,' said Gaskett, 'and that Dodds man at the Glebe Farm was screaming abuse at his dog, or the sheep, or both. He's absolutely mad. Heavens, it was diabolical, very embarrassing too. The vicar didn't know what to say . . . kept crossing himself, and looking up for guidance . . .!'

'Never mind about that,' snarled Foxie. 'Does anyone know how to switch that gun off? Is it dangerous? Do you have to approach it from behind? – I don't know. I'm gonna ring Clartiehole again – I'll get that lazy sod out of bed, if it's the last thing I ever do . . .!'

He grabbed the wall phone from its bracket and punched in the familiar numbers. Nothing. He looked at the gadget angrily, as if it was being unreasonable, tapped the cradle . . . and tried BT faults on 151. Silence. 'The bloody phones are off now,' he growled. 'Dead!'

'Perhaps that gun shot the line down,' suggested Beeday.

'Don't be ridiculous.' The QC was donning his pale blue wellies.

'C'mon,' he shouted. 'Let's find this weapon and dis-arm the damn thing. We'll deal with old Septimus in the morning.'

CHAPTER NINE

At 11.30 pm on the dot, James quietly withdrew his left arm from under Gloria's slumbering body, got out of bed and went to the bathroom. She heard the toilet flush, the shower running, and the buzz of an electric razor. When he came back into the room, a towel wrapped round his middle, hair wet, she asked, 'Aren't you staying for breakfast?'

He smiled, drying himself very thoroughly. He had a slight tan, looked very fit. Indeed he was, she could vouch for that. ''Fraid not,' he said quietly, as if concerned he might wake someone at this hour. 'I have to go. . . .'

Dressing now, casually smart, he checked he hadn't left anything behind . . . cigarettes, lighter, anything. 'Don't get up,' he said, 'I can see myself out . . . see y' sometime maybe.'

'I doubt it somehow,' said Gloria, with just a smidgen of

regret. She wasn't entirely convinced this had been simply a chance encounter. It had all been a bit too . . . she wasn't sure what . . . scheduled perhaps . . .? Arriving just as she got back from work, one phone call, coffee, drinks, seduction . . . a quick shower, and off he goes before midnight. It seemed almost programmed.

In the little conversation they'd had, he'd given nothing away. James, no surname, of no fixed address, no phone number. . . . Worked for a London firm of couriers, or so he said. Maybe. She got up, put on a robe and made instant coffee, watched him drink it, and kissed a fond goodbye. She saw the Mondeo reverse out onto the road, and he waved as it turned left, and quietly glided westwards over the bridge that crossed the Marleyburn, out of the village. It was cold, and Gloria quickly closed the door. She was pretty sure she'd never see him again. Pity.

James stopped a mile up the road, switched off the lights, opened a gate leading into a field, and reversed out of sight behind the hedge. From the boot, he donned dark blue boiler suit, boots, gloves and woollen hat. From the well under the spare he unearthed the jack-kit wrapped in a black plastic pouch. Among the limited array of tools, he found what he was looking for, checked it, and pushed it into his pocket. Then, after quietly replacing everything else and closing the lid, he stood silently for fully five minutes . . . before moving off along the fence. His footsteps made no sound on the grass. There was no passing traffic on this remote country road. He was alone on a cold damp March night, at nearly midnight, and that suited him fine. Another twenty minutes at the most, and he'd be away from Haugh House . . . mission completed.

* * *

Two hours earlier on the same evening, the gang of four met in the back room of 88 Armstrong Street, armed with pizzas and a can of coke each. That was to be their limit tonight. They had a mission too. Wally and Sol had arrived in the blue van nicked from the hospital car park three days ago, and kept out of sight since then. Wally had picked it up just after dark. It hadn't changed much. There were hundreds just like it all over town. All it needed was a change of plates to H reg., and a thorough clean out.

At 10.30 they loaded it up with the gear . . . overalls, balaclavas, Kevin's tool kit, two baseball bats . . . and the twelve bore from under the floorboards, still wrapped in sacking. Wally drove, Gazza in the front seat, the other two in the back. Joe was waiting for them at the lock-up. He opened the big wooden doors, switched the lights on, and there was the white transit . . . the unmistakable BT logo on both sides now. No evidence of Smithson's catering services or the cartoon chef on the back. A roof rack had been added with an extending ladder. It was a telephone repair van – a common enough sight anywhere.

Kev would drive this machine with Sol 'riding shotgun'. They laughed about that. 'Get 'em up and move 'em out,' said Gazza. 'Time to hit the trail boys. . . .' Joe wished them luck, locked his shed and went home. He had no idea where they were going, and he didn't want to know. Gazza had talked about easy pickin's out of town somewhere, but this caper looked to be more than your average Monday night semi-detached burglary. The plans, the two vans, four villains, special requests for paint job . . . uniforms, masks and sticks. . . . It had to be a major operation. This was like a mini task force about to descend on some unsuspecting island. No doubt he'd hear all about it in due course. Meanwhile time for bed. . . .

Twenty-five miles away, the good people of Hindburn, totally oblivious of the impending attack, were settling down for the night as well . . . in their various ways.

CHAPTER TEN

Miss Angela Fenwicke-Browne, well wrapped up against the cold, her little face barely visible inside a duffle coat, took her yappy little border terriers for their last ablutions. They knew perfectly well what was expected of them ... down to the bottom of the drive, some preliminary sniffing along the grass verge, and then squat. 'Come on you two, get on with it ... I'm not standing here all night. . . .' She said the same thing every night. It was part of the routine. She was a lady of routines and habits and disciplines, which were continued when they got back to the Hall. Dogs to their basket in the kitchen, hot chocolate drink, made with half milk half water, two rich tea biscuits ... take the phone off the hook, lock the doors ... and so to bed with Catherine Cookson perhaps. Certainly nothing too racy. Angela had only recently 'discovered' this author, who poured out a seemingly endless supply of romantic tales, which often reminded her of days gone by . . . when the Hall was full of noise and chattering. She could only just recall those times before the war. Were the summer days really warmer then? Were the winters always bright and white? Did everyone behave so much better – or was that just the simple colouring book of childhood? Undoubtedly the memories were happy.

Father in checky tweed suit, watch chain vanishing into a waistcoat pocket, pipe billowing smoke under a grey moustache – limping slightly as he crossed the lawn. A faded photograph on the piano still, taken while he was on leave in 1917, little more than a boy. Later he came home to join the family firm in the Newcastle office. Mining Engineers, coal (Classic Cookson) – and met mother at a Ball in the Royal Station Hotel, Christmas '28. Sometimes, when shopping in Newcastle, Angela would go there for lunch, and try to picture the scene. White tie and tails, long evening gowns, champagne in long-stemmed glasses, marking one's card for the valeta. . . . Standing to attention as the band played God Save the King after the last waltz. And then perhaps hurried whispered arrangements to meet again soon.

There were wedding photographs too, in a vast leather-bound album. Father tall, straight and rather serious. Mamma quite short and plump, and beaming, standing outside Hexham Abbey on a fine spring morning a year later.

There were two daughters, no sons. Angela's elder sister Catherine married a stockbroker from Bucks . . . four children, all grown up now of course. They still talked on the phone each weekend, taking turns to ring. . . . Two old ladies miles apart, but close. She remembered the two of them running along the passages in the Hall, playing hide-and-seek, friends for afternoon tea, building snowmen in the garden. The Hunt meeting in a blaze of scarlet in front of the house on winter days. Stirrup cups carried out by the servants – loud county voices, ladies perched side-saddle on prancing horses. Cheeky village boys teasing . . . old men touching the peaks of their caps in a respectful salute. Yesterday's sketches.

Miss Angela lay there in her cotton nightie, cardigan buttoned up around the neck, the novel upside down on her lap, sipping at the tepid chocolate . . . and played with such reflections in her mind.

Sad really. Here she was rattling about in this enormous house like a pea in a drum. All the fine furnishings still in place, pictures on the walls, crockery and cutlery in the cupboards . . . everything a little dusty perhaps, signs of a decaying elegance maybe. And yet it was all still there, the mess and memorabilia of several lifetimes, scattered about the rooms and passageways, upstairs and down. And one little old lady with her dogs.

It could have been different, might've been. Oh, she'd had her moments. Not many mind you . . . she'd never been the belle of the ball, the deb of the year, the flavour of the month. Too shy, too short, too 'countryfied' perhaps. Too late now. There had only ever been one *real* 'fling'. That holiday in the Lake District, early sixties. Bernard had been staying at the same hotel as Angela and her mother. For two glorious weeks they'd walked and talked, closer and closer, until on the last night she'd crept along to his room and lain there till dawn. They met several times after that, weekends in London, a dinner somewhere when he was up north. He even stayed at the Hall once. But somehow it just fizzled out, cooled off. Maybe she didn't try hard enough – or perhaps there was another more elegant woman nearer home? More accessible, more fun, younger, prettier. There probably was . . . you know what men are like, she smiled.

From time to time she saw his name. He'd become quite famous. A writer of epic historical novels, filled with dashing blades and heaving bosoms. Perhaps, Angela thought wistfully, she had been no more than a piece of early 'research'.

She yawned, turned out the light, and snuggled down into the duvet. She didn't often feel lonely, but tonight she did . . . just a little. She didn't know she was about to have visitors.

* * *

Just a few hundred yards away, over the fields, Gordon Graham was still playing with his computer, Shelagh fast asleep upstairs. There was no point in him going to bed until that damned church clock declared midnight . . . might as well do a little work on his investments. End of year coming up, capital gains to assess, top up the pension scheme perhaps. He poured himself a third small whisky from the bottle on the bureau, went back to the desk, and looked at his watch. Ten to twelve.

He wished he could sleep like Shelagh. That woman could nod off on a barbed wire fence, anytime. And the children were pretty good at it too. Maybe teenagers burned up more energy, needed more sleep to replenish hormones or whatever. Maybe . . . but he found it hard to accept. They must burn it all somewhere else, because neither of them displayed much enthusiasm for life at home, that was obvious. Young Stuart dragged his spotty gangly sullen body about the house, as if trailing one of Geordie Dodds's dead sheep. It didn't stop the miserable wretch eating like a rhinoceros though, did it? Then there were those long hours spent in his room listening to tuneless tapes and videos played at a trillion decibels. A cacophony of electronic riffs and angry rap, that made the old vicarage shake, and hold its head in disbelief. Did he ever do any homework up there? How could he, with such a racket going on? Would the layabout ever grow up and get a job? It certainly didn't look very promising at this stage – meanwhile the school fees were absolutely crippling! If Shelagh wasn't still working at the hospital, they could never afford this fancy boarding school education. Was it worth it? Probably not, thought Gordon – but look at it this way . . . if the kids had to go to the comprehensive, it would be a total disaster! They'd be at home all the time. God forbid!

And daughter Victoria was no better. When she came home, she only contrived to wallow in a permanent state of dogged, miserable boredom. In fact boredom became her irrational excuse for doing less and less. The entire holidays were spent lying about looking pale and gloomy . . . trance-like.

Shelagh, with her little bit of medical experience, would ask, 'Are you alright dear?' She might well have to ask *twice*, before extracting any sort of listless response.

'What?'

'You don't look very well darling . . . a touch of flu perhaps. There's a lot of it about. . . . Can I get you any-thing?'

'Eh? No, don't be ridiculous mother . . . it's nothing. You wouldn't understand. . . .'

Gordon certainly didn't. He lived with a wife who would rather be in the city, and two dull teenagers who made little effort to disguise their own disillusionment at living on the edge of the world, in a seventeenth-century barn, sur-rounded by grave stones and dumb animals. A teenage hell!

He sipped at his malt whisky, listening for the clock. Was this just a difficult stage all fathers went through? he wondered . . . or would it get even worse? Already, he realised, there were some alarming signs, especially with

Victoria. The little giggly creature in ankle socks had already metamorphosed into a complex moody nubile with attitudes and acne. He wasn't sure he knew how to deal with that.

At least it would probably be less traumatic with Stuart. Boys were more predictable weren't they? Less complicated. But it might not be long before he staggered home drunk from some teenage orgy, and was sick on the landing. That would be the beginning. After that there'd be a succession of crashed motorcars and visits from the police, and massive insurance premiums. The whole sordid parental picture was unfolding before his tired eyes. No bloody wonder he couldn't sleep!

*　*　*

Luckily all the double glazed windows at Paddock House were firmly closed, otherwise Donald and Diana might have roused half the parish. The Peabodys were having a major 'domestic difference'. It had begun shortly after the nine o'clock news . . . three nights ago.

It was born silently (as it always was) of something immensely trivial. A loo seat left up (again) . . . another coffee cup stain on the recently polished sideboard . . . a pair of unwashed underpants and one fetid sock draped fetchingly over the bannister. The sinister hush had fermented and simmered through a couple of sleepless nights for one, while the other lay snoring like a pig. It festered through a sniggering forty-minute phone call to Diana's sister in New Zealand, and inspired groans of disbelief when Donald used all the hot water having a bath.

This evening, it had exploded like a barrow load of Semtex when Diana found herself overwhelmed while trying to feed their seven emaciated Swaledales and the two potbellied Ayrshire bullocks, who inhabited the sea of clarts in the little paddock behind the house. The unhappy lady had the paper bag of protein pellets torn from her grasp. She was buffeted to the ground and unceremoniously trampled underfoot . . . until she lay there in the mud, skirt up around her neck, knickers wet, hair like a Rastafarian, one wellie and the bobble hat gone . . . screaming!

She had still been screaming when pompous Donald drove into the yard at seven-thirty in his spotless Jaguar, strode over in his immaculate legal suit, carrying his shiny new briefcase and said, 'Who the hell are you . . . and what on earth do you think you're doing sitting howling like a banshee on my doorstep??? Go away at once!!'

'I want you to get rid of those bloody awful creatures', she howled, 'I've had enough, I hate them – they're all mad!'

Donald looked stunned. 'Good heavens,' he said. 'It's *you*!'

'Sell them,' shouted Diana. 'Sell the land for building – make it into a golf course . . . give it to the gypsies, anything . . . I'm going back to work!'

And it was 'work' they were still arguing about now. Diana was determined. She was fed up looking like a damp battered bondager every day. Each time she fed the crazy ravenous beasts, she risked serious injury. It couldn't go on! Donald was equally determined his little woman should be at home to look after him . . . and the animals. They were an integral part of his country image . . . along with the 4-litre XJS of course.

Eventually, sometime after midnight, Diana picked up the carving knife and stormed out of the house. 'Good God, you're not going to slaughter the poor things, are you?' Donald yelled after her.

She didn't answer, but put her soggy wellies on again, and dragged a bale of hay down to the croft. She cut the strings, and threw the fodder over the fence. 'That's the last bloody feed you get from me!' she shouted, as they swooped on the unexpected late night snack. 'From now on you're on your own. . . . *Do you understand*??'

As she turned back to the house, she could see the lights shining in Mr Dodds's shed . . . and what appeared to be a BT repair van driving quietly through the village.

* * *

Across the road, Geordie found it hard to stay awake. Perhaps he could snatch an hour's respite before the next mule lambed. She'd begun to display the restless uneasy signs of impending motherhood, but there was nothing 'showing' yet. Time for a mug of tea and forty winks by the kitchen fire. Geordie was good at that. He was getting better as he got older. He left his wellies just inside the back door, as the church clock began its midnight call, and switched the kettle on. A half-perished lamb in a cardboard box by the hearth raised his head, stood up shakily and began to piddle. 'Ah well now bonnie lad,' said Geordie. 'Looks like y' might survive after all . . . do y' fancy some supper?'

He picked up the wobbly patient by the front legs to look at his belly, and saw the lamb was reasonably full. D'reen baby must've fed him before she went to bed. Geordie slumped into his chair, leaned forward and poked the fire into flame, and settled back staring at it, cup in hand, eyelids heavy. Half an hour would do. He'd feel better after that.

* * *

Jack and Nora at the pub had almost finished clearing up. There'd been a big crowd in tonight, big for a Monday anyway. The local trade was pretty steady, but some nights you got an unexpected rush of outsiders demanding four-course dinners and a wine list. The White Hart was hardly the place for that, but Nora could rustle up a good steak and chips, or a shepherd's pie . . . that sort of thing, value for money, nowt fancy. They'd fed a busload of pensioners coming back from a wet day trip to Ullswater, and they had seemed pleased enough with their grub. They drank a fair bit too, especially as none of them were driving. They stayed late.

The glasses were all washed, ashtrays emptied, tables wiped down, a quick run around with the vacuum. It was always easier to do it on the night. Leave it till the next morning, and it smelled disgusting. Even after twenty-five years in the business, neither of them had ever come to terms with the stale, smoky, beery smell. Jack had even given up the weed in '89, only an occasional cigar now . . . and tonight the bar seemed worse than usual. A lot of pipe smokers among the old men, who hadn't been allowed to light up on the bus. They'd made up for it in the pub though. The haze was still hanging there.

'I think we'll risk leaving a window open,' he said. 'Let some of this stour out. . . .'

It would be the last time he did *that* for a while.

CHAPTER ELEVEN

On that Monday, Giles Pollock took three calls from the London office, and a couple of faxes from Brussels. Everything seemed to be in order. No alarms, business as usual. He ate some cold beef for lunch, read through the *FT*, dozed in the chair, washed the car.

It was almost supper time when, purely by chance, he noticed the green flashing light on the answerphone. He pressed the button and heard a voice in very good English say, 'The head gardener is very angry. The bunnies are eating his lettuce. . . .'

He allowed the tape to run on, staring at the machine, but there was nothing else. Giles ran it back and played it again, and realised he was sweating a little now. He pressed another button to give him the caller's number. 00392 . . . followed by a jumble of figures that didn't matter. He recognised the first five readily enough: *Milan*!

God, not already, surely. Only yesterday, when he'd gone for the Sunday papers, had a drink in the Hart, he'd been thinking about his options, calling it a day. He'd made the decision, but now, *suddenly*, it was time to run! The message was from Arturo – there was no doubt about that. They'd always had this private arrangement. The first man to see the danger signals would call the other immediately – and they'd split. If he was lucky, Giles might get one more call to confirm, but he had no intention of waiting for it. He knew how these people worked . . . Arturo could do whatever he liked, bluff it out, or whatever. Giles was leaving *now*! He had hoped there might be more time, but no – this was definitely it. They might even be on their way already . . . or waiting for him somewhere when he flew back. Should he phone Marianne? They probably knew all about her. Her phone would be tapped. They might even be watching him at this very minute. He tried to recall faces in the pub, but other than the farmers, they were all strangers. He tried to convince himself he was worrying too much, too early. They would surely never try anything in a sleepy English village would they? Such crimes were unheard of here. No, they'd go for him in a crowd abroad some place. He was expected in Rome tomorrow or Wednesday . . . that's where they'd make their move, on their own turf. Maybe they didn't even know that he knew – yet. Maybe he still had a little breathing space – but he found he wasn't breathing too easily.

Polly shouted, 'Supper's ready,' twice before he answered.

'No thanks,' he called, 'haven't time, work to do, flight to catch in the morning . . . be gone a few days. . . .' Then as an afterthought, he added, 'Sorry dear.'

He locked the office door and began to pack the things he'd need. Bank documents, bond certificates, pass books, currency . . . Deutchsmarks and dollars, as well as a little sterling ... twenty-five thousand quids' worth in all. Passports (three of them), driving licences, credit cards, insurances, life policies ... everything was stuffed into one small holdall, and covered with a couple of spare shirts – strapped and padlocked ... hand luggage. He would buy a ticket at the airport, pay cash. He laid out an old navy sweater, a pair of slate grey slacks, and a blue and white anorak he'd bought for a skiing holiday years ago. If anyone was looking for him, they'd expect to see a businessman in a suit, with a briefcase and fancy luggage – his usual elegant self – not a tourist with one little bag. And it would all save time at the airport. He'd drive to Glasgow, fly from there. ... Anywhere would do for a start ... then try to leave no footprints.

At eleven o'clock he heard Polly go up to bed, and by then he was beginning to feel a little better, almost back in control of things. He had no plans to say goodbye, or leave a note. He would slip out quietly around midnight, and never be seen in Hindburn again. He went through to the lounge and poured himself a drink ... thought of Marianne lying on the beach in Durban ... and waited until he figured Polly would be asleep. He felt confident he was ahead of the game ... but maybe only just.

He was in the garage when the midnight call came, so he didn't hear the phone ringing.

* * *

Polly couldn't sleep. She heard it.

Strange, wasn't it? When Giles was away on business she slept like a log, no problem ... no pills. But when he was at home she felt uneasy, restless. It didn't make sense really. One might imagine she'd feel more vulnerable when alone, stuck out here miles from anyone, in a great big country house. But somehow it didn't work like that.

Certainly she didn't miss his 'stimulating' company

anymore. As far as Polly was concerned the marriage was at an end. If it wasn't for this lovely old house and the green fields all around, she would have left the pompous creature long since. But the idea of scuttling back to suburbia, even with a sackful of alimony, had no appeal. She would dig her toes in here. Hindburn was home now.

This weekend Giles was back from the continent again. He was downstairs now, nearly midnight . . . probably still wheeling and dealing, or counting his 'funny money'.

Oh yes, it had all been very exciting in the early days – she would admit to that. Nice house, some land, and a few peculiar animals to look after. Rare breeds, but just charming pets really, never remotely commercial. Still, they were fun, and kept her busy while Giles was off in his distant devious world. Brussels, Rome, Luxembourg . . . wherever . . . 'riding the gravy train,' he said. She was never sure what he actually did . . . never had been – not even when he was building Applepeel Electronics, and had something like a normal job. After the insider trading thing, he'd eventually moved on to be a 'Euro-consultant' . . . whatever that was. 'Just making use of all my old connections,' he would smile. 'Guiding a few people in the right direction . . . advisory work really. It's an absolute jungle out there darling – but there's money growing on trees, believe me. Seems only reasonable we should gobble some of it up – don't you agree . . .?'

Sometimes she would overhear intriguing telephone conversations. Generally from one end, of course, but on a few occasions she'd gently picked up the bedside phone, and listened . . . hardly daring to breathe. Often the talk was in French or Italian or Spanish (Giles was more than comfortable in all three languages . . . and German too) – and she barely understood a word. However when the dialogue was in English, all kinds of fascinating scenarios emerged. Substantial sums of money were often quoted ... EEC money, ECUs, Marks, Francs, Lire, anything. Whether any of this business was legal, or criminal – or simply a matter of taking advantage of a system ripe for usury – she couldn't be sure. But she knew Giles, and she guessed he would probably be into something dodgy. It was in the very nature of the man.

Whenever he came home for a day or two, the business usually continued. A stream of faxes would flow back and forth across the channel. Sometimes she might even find a few crumpled dispatches in the bin after he'd gone. Various funds would be quoted – the Social Fund, the Structure Fund, the Euro Agriculture and Guarantee Fund. Assorted banks and committees were mentioned – the Budgetary Control Committee, the Audit Committee ... the Euro Investment Bank, the Bank of Reconstruction and Development. It seemed his whole world was an impenetrable maze filled with shadowy deals, and lots of officials and bureaucrats who flitted from one ivory tower to another ... all apparently living on bottomless expense accounts. Eventually it became obvious, even to naive little Polly, that Giles had to be a cog (just how big she couldn't tell) in some massive fiddling machine. Maybe he'd even end up in prison again ... a little longer this time perhaps. Or was he still too shifty to be actually nailed down?

One time she picked up the phone, expecting a call from Diana Peabody at the Paddock ... invitation to coffee and a little local gossip ... but it was a Signor Luciano from Rome, clear as a bell, beautiful voice. Giles was in the garden, which was unusual. He was generally sitting waiting for these special connections, obviously pre-arranged ... and while she went to fetch her husband, Polly found herself wondering if this caller could be one of 'Lucky's' relatives ... a grandson perhaps? She'd become convinced the Mafia was involved somewhere along the line. Who else would be operating on such a scale? She'd probably discover a horse's head in her bed one of these nights.

On that occasion she'd hovered in the hall to eavesdrop.

'No problem,' she heard Giles say. 'Our man will put his squiggly signature and the official green stamp on the document first thing tomorrow. We'll have the funds into our account before the end of the month. In fact, as you're no doubt aware, the Control Committee are eager to be rid of the cash as soon as possible. If they don't manage to spend it soon, next year's budget will be reduced accordingly. Nobody gives a damn where it goes. Just get one of our boys to compile some convincing estimates. It could be a decade before anyone checks it out, and we'll be long gone by then, eh? Arrivederci Signor.'

Tonight, when the phone rang at midnight, Polly was in bed engrossed in Jilly Cooper. 'To hell with it,' she thought. 'It would be one of those Euro-creeps for Giles. He was probably waiting for the call.' She was warm, the book was easy reading, there was still a little Chablis in the glass. She wasn't going to move.

But a slow creeping curiosity got the better of her. She just had a sneaking feeling it might be something really interesting. Maybe one of Giles's cronies had been run over by that gravy train. That might not be such a great disaster, come to think of it.

By the time she stretched for her bedside phone it had stopped on the fifth ring. She stared at it for a moment or two, and returned to her book ... but found she wasn't really digesting the words anymore ... the sound of the phone still playing in her head. Had Giles answered it? Or was there a message on the machine?

Downstairs there was no sign of her husband. Perhaps he'd gone for a breath of fresh air. At this time of night? Not very likely. Maybe the phone call had taken him off to the airport already. He would just go. There might be a note somewhere, but that wasn't likely either. She pressed the playback button and heard Giles's silly little speech (he always enjoyed the sound of his own voice) . . . the bleep, and then the stark message. 'The rabbit catcher has been informed.' What on earth did that mean? It sounded rather ominous. Was some troublesome little varmint about to be snared perhaps . . .?

She couldn't find a note, and the clean white Merc was still in the garage. Strange! Where the hell was he?

CHAPTER TWELVE

Lucy Forbes-Robertson had 'floated' into the village about four years ago, and charmed Miss Angela into renting her the old schoolmaster's house opposite Glebe Farm. Angela's father had bought it in the late sixties, when the C. of E. primary was eventually closed, and the seven remaining country kids bussed into town. That was when the Fenwicke-Brownes still had three farms in their 'empire', and needed an estate worker to maintain the property. The last fella died there in '89. Since then, the house had been let to Mr and Mrs Flood (ex-Water Board man) but as they became rather doddery, and couldn't drive any more – the old couple had gone back to live in Newcastle to be nearer their daughter.

Perhaps Angela might have sold it then, to someone who fancied a yuppie nest in the country with a thatched bird-table, growing their own broccoli, but it was a listed building, dating back to 1750 or thereabouts, and probably too small for a posh family home anyway. Certainly there was no chance of planning permission to change it. So when her agent suggested it was worth a considerable amount to rent again, she agreed readily enough. There were short term arrangements now, much less of a problem to remove a troublesome tenant. . . . There were lots of respectable businessmen on six-month or one-year contracts moving up north these days, looking for a nice little rural pad within easy reach of Newcastle. It would have to be furnished, of course, but it could fetch over £500 a month. It seemed a good idea, and the subsequent 'ad.' created plenty of interest. The house might well have gone to an accountant with Northern Electric, an agreeable lad in software, a marketing man with a Japanese electronics firm. However, out of a bright blue Volkswagen Caravanette, with colourful flowers and butterflies painted all over it, came the large fluttering figure of Lucy.

The two ladies hit it off immediately. Lucy bypassed the agent and went straight to the Hall. She'd seen the notice board purely by chance, when she stopped for petrol at the garage . . . and promptly decided she had to have it. It was fate, destiny, kismet. Hindburn was where she was supposed to be. No more wandering.

When Miss Angela first saw the vivid van spluttering up her drive, she feared an imminent invasion of 'travellers' . . . litter, loud music, appalling behaviour, idle scroungers abluting behind the hedge. 'Ye gods, not in my back yard,' she thought, and promptly dispatched the terriers to repel the menace.

However Lucy was not in the least intimidated, in fact the dogs seemed to take an immediate liking to the visitor, as she sailed up to the front door in a vast billowing orange frock, and open toed sandals. She had a bottle of cheap red wine in one hand, and a bunch of daffodils in the other . . . long blonde hair falling about rosy cheeks, and a toothy grin. 'Lucy Forbes-Robertson,' she beamed. 'I believe you knew my father. Bernard writes truly appalling rubbish, but the books sell like lottery tickets . . . one or two even made into films. He often talks about *you*.'

After that, any other potential tenant had no chance. The two women drank the wine, talked of Bernard in particular, and men in general . . . and came to the conclusion that, like caviar and champagne, they could nicely live without them. That very afternoon the contents of the Caravanette were duly transferred to the School House, and Lucy settled in to become the cultural core of the parish.

The lady was an artist. Though it has to be said that when the locals were invited to view her vast surreal canvases, daubed with obscure shapes and lurid colours, some were less than convinced. 'What the hell is that supposed to be?' Geordie asked, staring blankly at 'Moonlight over Hindhope'. . . . 'Where's the church?' Lucy, her enthusiasm quite unaffected, would launch into a deep impenetrable diatribe on 'images beyond reality, the confusions of the mind, divine madness, fragments of the dream world' . . . and point out a spiky ultramarine and crimson splodge left of centre. 'Are you totally blind?' she enquired, quite genuinely concerned.

Lucy sculpted as well. Weird abstract objects, modelled in clay, fired in her oven, and then brightly painted. They were inspired, she claimed, by 'the very essence of nature all around'.

'It's a ewe,' she said, smiling at Sep's puzzled expression. 'Surely *you* of all people can recognise that . . . I was led to believe you were something of an expert on ewes.'

'We've got 325,' said Sep, 'and I'd have to admit there's a few funny buggers among them – but thank God none of

101

them look as poorly as this. Where's her lugs?'

It's the naked lovers,' she explained cheerily to Tommy Cleghorn, as he wandered round and round the copulating lumps, scratching his head. 'Which one's the woman?' he wanted to know.

'Come along Tommy,' she laughed. 'You're joking of course. . . .'

'Well t' be honest, it hardly matters,' said Tommy, 'cos I canna really fancy either o' them!'

Nevertheless, if Lucy's artistic talents were not always appreciated, her fervour knew no bounds, and with some help from Daddy's royalties, and a grant from the Arts Council, she opened her gallery and craft shop. Her very first sale was to Miss Angela. A confusion of grotesque gnome-like figures, which (when it was explained to her what the beasts were doing) Angela promptly placed behind the old stables in a bed of nettles – out of sight.

Tourists called, attracted by the riot of colour in an otherwise rather dull village street. They bought misshapen mugs, garish pots, unfathomable pictures . . . and usually left considerably poorer, with uncertain expressions. All, that is, except for an American from Pittsburgh 'doing' Europe in two weeks, who became convinced he'd fallen on something quite unique, a sort of female Dali. Perhaps he had. Anyway he cleaned out her entire stock. Geordie wasn't sure who was crazier – Lucy or the Yank.

She began writing poetry when she came upon a dead yow. She claimed it was the carcase, and the attendant crow that inspired her into verse.

> Alas what crueller fate at birth
> to witness mother die
> and watch black predator for all he's worth
> pluck out the glazed unseeing eye. . . .

> What heartless bird is this to steal
> what dark and feathered wit
> could so enjoy his evening meal
> before the lamb has found the tit. . . .

Other epics followed – some even worse . . . and as the merest suspicions of spring appeared, the lady began to drift about the fields and hedgerows, day and night, composing odes to rocks, thistles, spuggies, snails, badgers . . . everything, anything that seduced her eager imagination.

And she discovered Willie, big strong countryfied Willie, with his bright weathered face, hands like shovels, broad shoulders and neat bum. She wanted to paint the man, fashion him in bronze. She pestered him to pose. He could keep his Y-fronts on if he wanted to – she'd just use her imagination. Lucy said she could visualise him like Michelangelo's David. It would be equally famous one day – stand in the Tate perhaps. 'Forbes-Robertson's Willie', for all the world to admire.

But Willie wasn't having any of that. In fact he was seriously embarrassed at the whole prospect. 'Got a wife and two bairns,' he protested. 'I'm not standin' starkers on a stool in your back kitchen – what would folks think. I wouldn't dare go back t' the mart, woman!'

Undeterred, Lucy took a series of photographs, and fashioned her own image of the lad. A strange effigy she claimed depicted Willie carrying an orphan lamb. 'The devoted Shepherd' she called it. Willie was hugely relieved to see it bore not the slightest resemblance to himself . . . or indeed anyone else he'd ever met. Furthermore the lamb was not a readily recognisable breed either. 'I would've knocked the poor little bugger on the head at birth,' said Willie.

Nevertheless, Lucy quickly became a well-known (albeit

eccentric) addition to the life of Hindburn. There were daily sightings of 'that arty-farty woman', as she flitted about the village in flowing frock and ethnic beads. With her long straggly hair, she looked rather like a big friendly witch. When not tending her shop, she was often to be found sitting painting in the middle of a field. It could be quite disconcerting for the likes of Sep or Geordie Dodds to suddenly come upon psychedelic Lucy drawing or composing verse, crouched behind a hedge. Sep was even worried she might do something really avant garde to one of their old yowes. Well, he'd read of another alleged artist down south who'd actually cut a sheep in half, and preserved the poor beast in a glass case full of formaldehyde. The divided carcase was even on display in a gallery somewhere – people queuing up to look at it. Would y' believe that? They must all be bonkers. Nevertheless he told Willie to keep an eye on Lucy, and if he ever caught sight of her carrying a chain saw anywhere on Clartiehole, to disarm the woman immediately!

* * *

On that busy Monday night, Lucy was sitting on a grave stone composing a sonnet to the spirits, when the BT van pulled up behind the trees beyond the churchyard. She was extremely annoyed by this intrusion. She had convinced herself that the only place to truly experience the appropriate muse was right here among the dear departed, *alone*. Gordon Graham from the vicarage had already disturbed her solitude. 'Can't sleep until after the midnight chimes,' he said. That was half an hour ago, and now, just as she was beginning to feel the merest murmurings of inspiration, the teeniest troubled tremblings from the tombs . . . here was this live telephone engineer on double overtime groping about in the dark! Damn the man!

She slid quietly down behind the mossy memorial to

'Arthur Edward Forster, 1749–1820 and his beloved wife Isobel 1752–1832', and silently cursed.

It was cold and damp among the stones. She had a great urge to stand up and flap about on the spot to keep warm . . . but that would surely discourage the slumbering spirits, and probably upset the Forsters too. It would almost certainly have induced an instant cardiac in young Kevin as well. The last thing he expected to see on this expedition was a weird wellied ghost dancing about in a graveyard!

So Lucy sat there shivering, waiting for the man to finish whatever he was doing and go away.

It was a week ago that Kev, with a little guidance from his pal Alistair in Telecom, had worked out which wires to cut. (It was worth a fifty and two tickets for the Liverpool match.) They'd tracked the cables from the local exchange building, and found the little junction box beneath the grass verge not far from the churchyard gate. A 'key' was needed to lift the lid and get at the maze inside. That was no problem. The secret was to cut off *only* the village, not half the bleedin' county. They knew BT fault-finding technology would pinpoint the damage soon enough, once it was reported . . . or some eager night shift operator sussed it out – but hopefully they'd do nowt till morning. As long as there were no frantic emergency calls out of Hindburn for an hour or two . . . that would do the trick. Yuppie Cellnets were no use here.

Sol watched his partner from the passenger seat of the transit, the old hammer action twelve bore lying over his knees, loaded. He was stroking it as if it were a pussy cat.

Kev came out of the hole, threw his bag of tools into the back and came into the cab. He lit a cigarette and looked at his watch. It was 12.32. Turning to Sol, he said, 'Are we ready then?'

'Ready.' Sol grinned.

'Okay, you know where we go first. A big house full of stuff, one little old woman, probably fast asleep, there shouldn't be any trouble. And you'll certainly not need that thing, so put it away!'

Sol nodded sullenly. He didn't like being ordered about, treated like a kid . . . but it happened all the time. They thought he was just the big thick heavy, but he reckoned he was as bright as any of them . . . 'cept maybe Gazza. 'Okay, let's go,' he grunted, and reluctantly pushed the gun back under the seat.

Lucy had watched the man crawling about in the grass. He'd fiddled there (doing something highly technical no doubt) for a couple of minutes. He was just a dark shape, that's all. She couldn't really see a face. She saw him put his bag into the van, saw the red cigarette glow in the cab, and watched it move away.

But by now her enthusiasm had all but evaporated, the humour, the mood destroyed. Instead a chill melancholy crept over the lady. It was no use staying out here – she'd talk to the ghosts some other night. Slowly she rose and made her way among the grave stones, through the creaking wrought iron gates, and out onto the road . . . Lucy headed home to her cosy little house, unaware of course that she had just witnessed the first act of Gazza's 'masterpiece'.

106

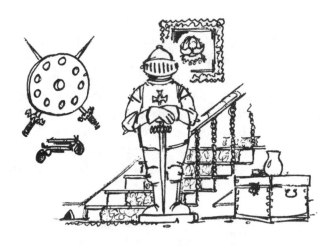

CHAPTER THIRTEEN

Kev switched off the lights as they turned into the driveway, and eased the van gently down the slight gradient to the Hall. The wheels made a worrying noise on the gravel, but the engine was barely ticking over in second gear. He stopped at the bend just before the house came into view, and reversing into the trees, performed a quiet 'tiptoe' turn. The transit now pointing out towards the road again . . . just in case they were forced to leave in a hurry. It was dark and drizzly. Sol rubbing his hands, feeling the cold dampness in the night air . . . eyes becoming used to the gloom.

They had already decided to get in quickly – see what the layout was, the geography of the place, and then reverse the van up to the big door and load. There was only one weak light glowing in the hallway, one eye in the shadowy square hulk of sandstone dozing among the big bare trees. It

107

had stood there in one shape or another for 350 years, arrogantly dismissive of anyone or anything likely to violate its solid superior position.

Going in through the massive oak door was not an option. It was almost six inches thick, and firmly locked. Part of Miss Angela's evening routine was always to push in the thick iron bolts top and bottom, after the last dog walkies. The back entrance into the scullery and kitchen would've been easier . . . quite simple in fact . . . a rather slim glass panelled door there – but Kev wanted everything out at the front, straight into the van. There were tall glass windows on either side of the porch, but they were probably reinforced and alarmed. They looked too vulnerable, too easy. A small frosted window to the right suggested a downstairs toilet, and Kev reckoned he could squeeze through that, if he removed his anorak. It probably led into the hallway. Wally had mentioned it after one of the reccies. He said *he* could get in easily.

Standing on a garden seat, Sol pressed the plunger securely onto the single pane, and removed the putty from around the frame. The window came out intact without a sound. The smaller of the two thieves clambered through head first, down onto the loo seat, and switched on his torch. There was a wash basin with ancient ornate brass taps, and a prehistoric privy complete with iron cistern set on high, and dangling chain. Nothing else. Cautiously opening the door he found, as predicted, it led out to a panelled foyer with polished parquet floor . . . and the main entrance at the far end. The bolts seemed to make an horrendous noise, the giant key screeched as it was turned, and the hinges squealed when the door was opened . . . to reveal Sol standing at the top of the steps, like a gigantic gnome. Entry had taken less than five minutes.

'Get the van here, quietly,' whispered Kevin, and turned

to shine a little light on what was available. Perhaps if things went well, if they weren't disturbed, he might risk the electricity later.

'God, it's a bloody museum,' he muttered to himself. The hall and all the way up the wide staircase, right onto the landing above, was walled in dark wood. A faded threadbare carpet led the way. There was a musty mouldy smell about – as if the house hadn't been lived in for years – but it was filled with the flotsam of its history. A suit of armour, both hands on the hilt of a rusty sword, stood sentry at the foot of the stairs. For the briefest of moments Kev imagined it was someone watching him. Everywhere, sombre pictures of bewhiskered gentry stared out from ornamental gilt frames. Muskets, swords, shields and antique pistols clung to the walls. Half way up the stairs, a small figure of a dusky native boy carrying a tray. He wore a turban, white waistcoat, voluminous red trousers, and a friendly grin. 'They're everywhere,' Kev thought. It reminded him of the kid in the Paki mini-market on the corner of Dunstan Avenue . . . open twenty hours a day.

Sol was already in the dining room emptying drawers of silverware, and making too much noise. 'Sssshhh,' Kev hissed, 'For Chrissake!'

'There isn't a telly,' said Sol sounding amazed. 'Or a video . . . nothing but knives and spoons in here. . . .'

'It's a bloody treasure trove, y' daft bugger,' Kev growled. 'Get the whole lot into the transit. And all those paintings as well. . . . That big silver bowl – it's worth a fortune. This cabinet's probably antique, Queen Anne or something. I'll give y' a lift in a minute. Fast as y' can. . . .'

He moved into the lounge on the other side of the passage, and was surprised to find how cosy it looked. A vast sofa you could nicely kip on. This, and three big armchairs dressed in colourful patterned material, but horse hair peeping out sadly from the shabby bodies underneath. An elegant room though, high panelled ceiling, a chandelier in the middle, lamps on tables in corners and alcoves, to give gentle intimate light. He switched on one of them, and a warm reddish glow spread about the room. A writing desk over by the window, the lid laid open, papers strewn about. He tried the top left hand drawer, and as luck would have it, found about a hundred quid in notes and loose change. Top right was locked, or stuck tight. Middle right revealed a cheque book, two building society pass books, and what appeared to be insurance documents of some sort. Company names he recognised. Five drawers wouldn't budge, and for a moment Kev considered forcing them open. He had the tools, but why bother . . . why not take the complete desk, or bureau, or whatever it was. He tried it for weight – Sol would probably tuck it under one arm.

He began taking down the pictures. A seascape over the mantlepiece was nice, he liked that. High angry waves tossing little ships about. It might even be the mouth of the Tyne. He could just read the artist's name . . . somebody called Carmichael was it? It meant nothing to Kev, but he took it out the front door.

His mate had virtually cleared the dining room. A mountain of silver, and more paintings stacked flat along the side of the van, a heavy wooden chest with brass handles, clasps and locks, jammed up against the art work, holding it all safe and secure for the journey back.

'I couldn't open the box,' said Sol, holding the great padlock in his hand. . . . 'Maybe it's full of gold . . . so I brought it.'

They carried the writing desk out too, and a glass fronted cabinet on spindly delicate legs. They both looked valuable. And more paintings . . . Benny the fence had said bring all the pictures from the big house. Maybe he knew what was in here, knew what they were worth. Kev remembered him talking about painters called Atkinson and Hedley. There was some of their stuff in the house apparently . . . maybe even a Turner, he said . . . whatever *that* was. Anyway, if it had ever been in the Hall, it was now in the van.

They cleared the two main rooms in double quick time. They'd done it before. Almost everything that wasn't nailed down was removed. They shifted a few antique items from the passageway, and moved on to what looked like a study or a den . . . with a vast roll top desk, framed photographs on top. Three walls lined with shelves holding ancient leather bound books, the fourth covered by sporting cartoons. There were trophies, cups and silver salvers on a sideboard. . . . 'Take them,' said Kev. He'd just picked up a gleaming figurine of a prancing stallion, when the dogs began to bark somewhere in the back of the house. At about the same time they heard the big front door slam shut.

For a moment the two villains stood motionless, hardly daring to breathe, just staring at each other. Kev was the first to move. He put down the stallion, and cautiously crept out into the passage, Sol towering over him, so close behind that they both saw the problem at the same time. A stocky, almost spherical figure was blocking the escape route. Clad in pale blue cotton nightie, green wellies and a khaki duffle coat . . . armed with a circular shield (late sixteenth century) and a very ugly looking rusty claymore . . . Miss Angela Fenwicke-Browne stood legs apart defying anyone to pass.

'Who the hell are *you*?' she demanded sternly.

'Shoot 'er,' said Kev, who had now changed places with his associate, and was peering out from under Sol's armpit.

'Is it a ghost?' asked Sol.

'Shoot the bitch,' Kevin hissed.

'You told me to leave the gun in the van,' Sol protested. 'What do we do now?'

'Just kill 'er,' screamed Kev, never taking his eyes off the apparition. 'Go on – strangle 'er!'

Sol, without total conviction, shuffled six inches forward, trying to look really savage, fists clenched, lip curled into what he imagined was a terrifying snarl. After all, he'd flattened many a heavy down the Bigg Market, thrown a few overweight drunks into the Tyne, cracked a few heads together . . . but *this* was a first.

'One step more and I'll run you through, you great fat pig,' growled Miss Angela, raising the heavy sword until the point was directed shakily at Sol's navel. The shield still covered the lady's heaving bosom and violently beating heart, but the expression from under the duffle coat hood suggested no chance of a compromise.

'We should've had the gun,' said Sol looking at his watch. 'We're supposed to be out of here by now.'

'We could rush 'er,' said Kev . . . but a twitch of the claymore dissuaded them.

It might have stayed this way for some time, an impasse, a stand-off . . . if it hadn't been for the intervention of the terriers. Suddenly the two yapping creatures emerged from the kitchen like a couple of hairy little missiles. Going so fast, they failed to negotiate the bend in the passage that led to the front door, and ricocheted off the panelled wall. Without pausing, legs still going at a million revolutions a minute . . . desperately trying to get some grip on the parquet floor . . . they gathered momentum again, and careered past the intruders before virtually disappearing up Miss Angela's nightgown.

Not surprisingly this completely threw the poor old lady off guard, and she dropped the sword. It was the chance Kevin had been waiting for. He pushed Sol towards the agitated woman screaming, 'Go on man, get 'er,' – and Sol, without much choice in the matter, lunged forward to

112

overwhelm the confusion of dogs and duffle coat. Miss Angela tried gamely to beat him off with the studded shield, like some rancid Reiver might have done 300 years ago . . . but Sol was far too big, too heavy. A glancing blow to the head had no effect on the monster, and the two of them tumbled to the floor, Sol on top, the old lady breathless below, Kev standing over them with the sword. The dogs, perhaps confused and disappointed at events, frantically extracted themselves from the chaos and, still yapping bravely, tore back along the passage to the refuge of their basket. Again they failed to take the corner satisfactorily.

'We'll tie her up,' said Kev. 'I've had enough of this, the woman's a bloody menace!' He got some cord from the van, and together the thieves strapped Miss Angela to the banisters. She fought like a tiger, but they were too much for her. Even if she freed herself eventually she couldn't phone anybody, couldn't raise the alarm . . . and it was a mile or more to the nearest house. The lads would be long gone by then.

'You should be horse-whipped,' she yelled defiantly as they collected the last of her treasures. 'Animals!'

Kev briefly considered chopping her head off with the rusty old sword, or at least giving her a good kick . . . but instead he just banged the door behind him, and left her sitting there at the bottom of the stairs . . . trussed up like a Christmas turkey.

CHAPTER FOURTEEN

Geordie Dodds actually saw the blue van drive into the vicarage yard. He was on his way over to the lambing shed for the umpteenth time. A busy night . . . two triplets, four pairs, and another ewe already in agitated mood. He wasn't finished yet.

But the van worried him. For a start it had no lights, it was a stranger . . . and what the hell was anybody doing at this hour – one o'clock in the morning! However, as he told Tommy Cleghorn later, it really wasn't any of his business, and he had enough on his plate already. He hadn't time to investigate – and maybe make a fool of himself. Perhaps it was something private. Mr Graham was often up and about late. But nevertheless he went back into the house and phoned the vicarage number. He felt he couldn't just ignore it. But the phone was off, not for the first time this winter. So that was that, wasn't it? He could concentrate on his sheep again, and by now there was no sign of the vehicle anyway. All quiet. Back to the 'maternity ward'.

Meanwhile, on the other side of the road, less than a hundred yards away, Gordon Graham, bleary-eyed, was watching a sexy movie on Sky, a cup of warm Horlicks clutched in both hands, dressing gown wrapped over striped pyjamas . . . sleep beckoning, but hardly insistent yet. Gazza and Wally could see him through the window. The patterns from the screen flickering on the ceiling, a table lamp glowing behind him, a magazine lying by his slippered feet. This one wouldn't be difficult.

Gordon was gawping dozily at a bevy of naked nubiles frolicking in a tropical lagoon, when two men in boiler suits and balaclavas burst into the room. He promptly spilled the Horlicks onto his lap and, as he began to stand up, Gazza belted him hard across the side of his head with a gloved fist . . . just to show the man this was serious business, no messin'. Gazza switched off the TV. 'Who else is in the house?' he growled right into Gordon's face. You had to scare the life out of them at square one . . . there was seldom any bother after that. A golden rule.

When the answer wasn't instant, Gazza hit him again. This time the victim went down in a heap, squealed, and put a hand up to his ringing ear. He was on all fours in front of the fireplace. 'Nobody,' said Gordon, then thinking better of it, he added weakly, 'Well my wife's upstairs in bed, probably asleep.'

Gazza looked over to Wally, and Wally disappeared up the stairs two at a time. Shelagh heard the footsteps coming, and wondered if the sexy movie had perhaps inspired her husband. Something had definitely roused *her*, but in her warm drowsy state, she wasn't sure what. By the time Wally came through the door she was sitting up with a silly grin on her face, trying to look provocative in curlers . . . a shoulder strap pushed seductively over a plump shoulder. When she first saw the shadowy figure in his burglar's gear, she briefly imagined Gordon might have gone a bit kinky . . . perhaps this was some strange new fetish he'd acquired. How exciting!

It was only when Wally growled, 'Giz yer jewels pet!' that she realised this was unlikely to be a romantic evening.

'Git up,' he snarled from behind his mask, and grabbing a handful of hair among the plastic rollers, dragged the petrified woman downstairs to join the boss.

A hurried search through the other rooms of the rambling old house, revealed no other occupants. 'The children are away at school,' Shelagh told them in a warbling voice. She was on the floor clinging to Gordon's knees, a blanket pulled up around her neck for warmth, protection, modesty . . . whatever. 'Take whatever you want,' she cried. She was wide awake now, and scared half to death. This was the worst possible nightmare. Here they were, huddled together in the middle of the night, miles from anywhere, surrounded by sheep – and at the mercy of two evil gangsters who would probably cut their throats and steal her 'Magimix'. It got worse.

A tap on the door heralded the arrival of Sol and Kevin. Gazza let them in. 'How'd it go?' he asked. 'Brilliant,' said Sol. 'The van's nearly full already. . . . We had to tie the old lady up though – she was a bit of a nuisance. . . .'

Sol was detailed to glower over Mr and Mrs Graham, while the other three ransacked the house. They removed the TV, video and the Sky unit first. They gathered up cutlery, ornaments and pictures from most of the rooms on the ground floor. They emptied Gordon's office of cash, credit cards, computer and anything else that looked remotely valuable. Kev and Wally even carried out a grandfather clock from the landing, the maker's name and date (1824) drawn on the colourful face. It tried to chime in protest as they laid it flat in the VW van.

Upstairs Shelagh's dressing table drawers were cleared of rings, necklaces, brooches, jewels and gems ... some bought in far away places while Gordon was abroad on business trips ... anniversary presents, and surprise gifts whenever he got a bonus from the firm. Others handed down from mother, granny, old maiden aunts. Priceless ... sentimental.

The thieves created havoc wherever they went. Weeks later when it was still an awful memory, Shelagh said the mess was almost worse than the robbery. The everyday order of the house had been shattered. True it had never been spotless ... she wasn't one of those fanatical houseproud women who vacuumed under beds, and dusted the spare room every week ... but at least you had a rough idea where everything was supposed to be. She had never pretended to like the big draughty building at the best of times. After that terrible night, she hated it ... couldn't wait to get out.

The gang completed their sacking of the vicarage in well under the hour. There were a few more violent threats about revealing a secret safe, but they found no evidence of such a thing. Gordon would certainly have told them readily enough. They left in high spirits, after locking the unfortunate Grahams in a cupboard under the stairs. Sol pushed a big heavy sideboard up against the door ... and left them there surrounded by brooms and buckets and old golf clubs, shivering in the dark.

* * *

Lucy Forbes-Robertson saw the four furtive figures on the village street as she came out of the bathroom. She had returned from the churchyard damp and cold to discover the fire dead in the grate, the whisky bottle empty – and decided to wallow in a hot bath before bed. It seemed the logical thing to do, even at this hour. In any case the clock rarely dictated Lucy's behaviour. She slept when weary, ate when hungry, and 'created' whenever the spirit entered her head. Visitors, customers, often found a sign on the shop door, 'Sorry, back soon.' It was unwise to wait. She might be gone a week.

Just why she looked out of the window at that particular moment she wasn't sure. It didn't matter . . . one of those impulsive things . . . maybe to see if it was still raining. And there in the gloom she saw them walking up the road towards the Pratt house. Was one of them the figure she'd seen down by the church? It could be . . . same shape. What the hell was going on? Who were they? What were they doing in Hindburn at two o'clock in the morning for God's sake? She flicked the switch on the kettle and dialled 999. Coffee and the police suddenly seemed a good idea. The kettle boiled and bubbled into life, but the phone was dead, not a sound. Lucy hurriedly began to get dressed again.

* * *

Gazza noticed the light in her window as they strolled past. The farm shed was still lit up, the bloke in the vicarage had been sitting watching telly at one o'clock in the morning when they walked in. Did nobody ever go to bed in this village?? At least he was relieved to see no signs of life at 'The Forge'. With a bit o' luck they'd get in and out of this one undisturbed. A quickie before the shop and the pub.

Actually getting into most houses presented no real problem. Kev had such an array of keys, and an assortment of tools, almost any domestic door could be breached. Only the most substantial bolted variety would defeat them. In any case, there was often another more vulnerable entrance. A window of opportunity somewhere.

The major inconvenience these days were the new sophisticated alarm systems, which some selfish unreasonable householders installed in and around their posh premises. At the Hall there had been nothing, Miss Angela having concluded the last thing she needed, stuck out in the country, miles from anybody, was a cacophony of jangling bells that no one but she would ever hear. The old vicarage boasted a system connected by phone line direct to the police station – but that had been taken care of by Kev's earlier exercise.

Here at 'The Forge', the gang were lucky. Trevor Pratt had installed powerful lights all around his new country property, activated whenever an intruder approached and broke the electronic beam. Inside the house another gadget triggered off a two-tone 'musical' alarm. Furthermore, whenever the family were away a time switch on selected lights and curtains would suggest to any casual observer that the Pratts must still be in residence. All clever stuff. The trouble with this subtle and sensitive 'show biz' combination of lights and music was that all sorts of wandering nocturnal wildlife could set it off. Suddenly in the dead of night the whole neighbourhood might be bathed in a trillion-watt halogen glow, and the family woken from their slumbers by the infuriating ding dong ding. All this because some smelly old tom cat was sniffing about in the rubbish bins.

After a few nights trying to sleep through something akin to a West End musical, Trevor had switched the technology off, and only turned it back on if the family were away from home. Of course Gazza couldn't know this, and Kev was duly sent in ahead to deal with the sensors. He quickly reported back that they weren't operating. It was a free ride.

There *was*, however, one small problem. What to do with the vans? It was a bit risky having *two* strange vehicles parked out on the village street. One was suspicious enough. The Hall had been nicely secluded, a mile down the lane . . . the vicarage hidden away in the trees – but 'The Forge' was right on the roadside, only a small paved forecourt leading to the garage and the green front door. Far too exposed. So Gazza had decided to leave both trucks in the vicarage garden, and walk to the Pratt place. He rather fancied the idea. It was just like that old western on the box . . . four desperados strolling down the street of Deadwood to rob the bank or the saloon. Alright, so maybe Gazza and the gang didn't have the proper hats, the boots, the spurs . . . but it was very cool. That's when Lucy saw them.

At the back of 'The Forge' was a small lean-to utility room, about nine feet by twelve. It looked as if it might have been added on as an afterthought . . . flat roof, small window, a cheap panelled door. Wally had this eased off the hinges in no more than a minute. Inside, space for the freezer, washing machine and a lot of horsey harness. Beyond was a more substantial entrance to the main body of the house. Locked – but at the fifth attempt one of Kev's keys turned it, and they were in.

They could see at once the family were at home. Dishes on the draining board by the sink, knickers draped on the radiator, school books lying about . . . the kitchen waste bin three-quarters full of culinary debris. Still a slight aroma of cooked supper and washing up liquid. And the dog. There was often a dog somewhere. They *could* be a real nuisance. Anything from the bossy little terriers they'd encountered at the Hall to the great man-eating Alsatian they'd met in Sunderland last month. They all seemed to take exception at being roused from their rabbit-chasing dreams, and usually felt obliged to wake up everybody else as well. Butch was different. Normally he might have been inspired to leap up and *lick* the intruders to death, but tonight he barely opened an eye. The tail twitched an unenthusiastic welcome, and he went back to sleep. To hell with it – the last thing he needed at his age was more midnight walkies! He'd done that.

The robbers moved out of the kitchen into the hallway, onto a thick quiet carpet which continued up the stairs, same pattern. Gazza pointed Sol to the top of the landing. His job was to ensure that there were no nasty surprises. No uninvited residents thoughtlessly interrupting the orderly removal of their valuables.

It all went very smoothly . . . no talking, no bumping into each other . . . Sol rather disappointed that no one came out of a bedroom and presented him with an excuse to blast a shot into the ceiling.

It was a good haul . . . more TV sets, another video, two radios, a microwave – in fact every electrical gadget they could carry was hauled out into the drive at the side of the house. As soon as it became apparent this was 'easy pickin's', Wally trotted over to the vicarage for one of the vans. Gazza and Kev continued to empty drawers and cupboards in all the downstairs rooms, filling sacks they'd brought with them, and some dirty pillow cases from the utility room. In Trevor's office they found a small metal safe, with combination lock, very heavy. With the help of Sol they dragged it away, to open later. Cash, cards, Trevor's fax, his PC and word processor were taken, and still no embarrassing interruptions. Gazza even considered moving upstairs for the jewellery, but figured it might be pushing their luck. No need to be greedy. Get the stuff loaded.

The second van was almost full as well now. After the safe and all the other goodies from inside the house, there was just room for the fridge, a washing machine and a girl's bicycle standing behind the broken door.

121

Excellent.

Three of the lads piled into the front of the blue van, Wally driving . . . and Gazza went back for the BT vehicle at the vicarage. He felt like Clint Eastwood. Four more hits, and they'd be outa here and back to the city before dawn.

CHAPTER FIFTEEN

Lucy was prepared for the worst. Hair stuffed into a black woolly bobble hat and pulled down over her ears . . . a shirt, two sweaters, tights, heavy blue corduroy trousers and Doc Martens. The whole 'provocative' ensemble covered by paint stained overalls and a Barbour coat. The lady was unlikely to suffer from exposure on this cold March night, and if one of those suspicious characters she'd seen sneaking about tried to molest her . . . she figured the poor man would be totally exhausted long before he fought his way to the private bits. In the murky light of night, she could easily be mistaken for a very substantial hill shepherd . . . not to be messed with.

She had decided not to bring a torch, and it took a few minutes to get used to the dark. . . . After that things began to take shape. She knew the geography of the village well enough, and most of the surrounding landscape too. This wasn't the first time Lucy had gone walkabout at night.

The lights in Geordie's shed still shone through the Yorkshire boarding, but there was neither sign nor sound from any other quarter. Hindburn *appeared* to be asleep. Maybe her romantic imagination had overreacted. Perhaps, after all, there was nothing sinister going on, maybe she was being foolish. Everybody thought she was pretty crazy anyway. . . . Nevertheless, she walked slowly and carefully past the old school, always keeping her body in the deeper shadows of a wall, a hedge, a tree . . . never out in the open. A dog barked somewhere, miles away. A branch groaned, complaining in the wind. Was that a fox screeching over towards Clartiehole? Then nothing. She stood for a moment, completely still. A worried ewe bleated in Geordie's croft. Quiet again.

When the crash came she almost wet herself. It wasn't because the noise was particularly loud – it probably didn't wake anybody . . . it was just such an alien, unexpected sound. It broke the peace, and before that could be repaired, the bell rang. Almost a merry jangling ring, determined it seemed to violate any lingering calm. It didn't last long, maybe five seconds, no more . . . but it left Lucy with the noise still in her head.

It took a little while to pull herself together, to reorganise her brain, realise what was happening. 'The shop! Of course – that's where they are. The devils are robbing the Post Office . . .!'

Suddenly excited, heart beating fifteen to the dozen, she hurried along the grass verge towards the White Hart. Fred and Doris's place was almost opposite – she'd be able to see what was going on from there. She was running, crouching low under the line of the stone wall, and nearly went too far . . . almost made a mess of it. Just in time she saw the BT van. It was standing under the trees in the pub car park, barely visible, a man leaning against the side smoking, waiting. Two more paces and he would've seen her.

She watched him stamp on his cigarette, check his watch, and look over towards the shop. She followed his gaze. 'Good God, there was another vehicle over there. Where did that come from? How many of these thieving scoundrels were there?'

This second van, similar shape, darker, with no markings that she could see, and no lights of course, was parked up beside Fred Little's garage. It was smartly tucked away off the road, but obviously ready to go. Another figure . . . no dammit, two of them, lurking between the van and the building. Any self-conscious doubts she might have harboured till then were surely dispelled now. It was all adding up . . . phones off, breaking glass, a brief alarm bell quickly silenced, two strange vans . . . and now a flickering torch light inside the Post Office. She could see it. She knew she'd been right all along. This had to be something really serious . . . but was she the only witness? Was she the only villager who knew what was happening?

Lucy was sweating. She wished she hadn't put so many clothes on. She was definitely overdressed for spying . . . and quite desperate for a pee. Luckily, so was the man in the car park. Perhaps out of habit, rather than any over-developed modesty, he turned away and pointed himself towards the hedge . . . and this gave Lucy a chance to dart across the road into the garden at 'The Forge', and through into Mr Pratt's small paddock. She stumbled a couple of times, banging her knee on a spade or something, but eventually scrambled out into the Marleyburn field behind the shop. From there she could get a better view of the dark van, and the big 'minder' guarding it. She could also see the back of Geordie's illuminated shed, and headed straight for that.

He was squirting iodine onto a red raw navel, the lamb held between his knees . . . syringes and bottles and pills on a nearby bale of straw. His stick hanging on a hurdle.

He looked up, startled as she came into the light, breathless and waving her arms. 'Mr Dodds, thank God you're still here,' she gasped. 'There's a robbery going on. . . . Is your phone alright, can I call the police . . . ?'

'The phone's knackered,' said Geordie. 'A robbery y' say – whereabouts?' He gave the lamb back to mother.

Lucy told him what she'd seen. The van at the church, the men walking up the village, the events at the Post Office. 'They're in there now!' she said.

'Y' know, I knew there was somethin' fishy happening!' said Geordie quietly. 'There's been some strange folk about lately, and I saw a van m'self earlier on . . . I wondered about it.' He pushed his cap back and rubbed his brow. 'There could be a few of them I suppose. . . . No good you 'n' me tacklin' them, that's for sure. We'll need reinforcements bonnie lass. . . .'

They went into the house where Lucy tried the phone again. Geordie got Doreen out of bed, and sent her across the road in her nightie to the kiosk. He suspected it might be useless too, and it was . . . but it was worth a try. By the time Lucy came out of the bathroom, feeling much better, and several items lighter, he had the pick-up keys in his hand. 'Go and get Willie,' he said, 'and maybe auld Sep as well – quick as y' can. Tell them there's an emergency!'

Doreen, who hadn't said a word, or even asked what all this commotion was about, was then detailed to rouse Tommy Cleghorn across the way, and fetch him here. 'Don't come back without 'im,' Geordie shouted as she trundled off tappy lappy over the road, covered in one of her husband's old coats now. The pockets were half full of staples, nails, nuts and bolts, and an old lamb's foot knife he claimed she'd thrown out with the refuse. At least the weight of all this agricultural debris kept the coat down in the wind. But it was still draughty around her knees . . . and the wellies felt cold and clammy without her socks on. She hoped Tommy was a light sleeper, so she could get home as quickly as possible.

In fact she was fortunate. Tommy was opening the door as she raised her hand to knock. He was in a moderate fettle – and about to 'sort out' Gordon Graham at the vicarage. The bloody man was a pest. God knows what he was up to, but it sounded as if he was demolishing the west wing. He'd been banging and howling for the last half hour. Didn't he realise what time it was? . . . Some people had to go to work tomorrow!

'Geordie says it's really serious,' pleaded Doreen. 'A matter of life 'n' death . . . he'll kill me if you don't come over straight away!'

* * *

At Clartiehole, Willie was dozing on the chair when Lucy burst in. For a terrible moment he thought the woman might be dangerously amorous, and quickly made sure he was 'properly dressed'. She certainly seemed seriously agitated.

'No time to talk,' she panted, 'Mr Dodds says come immediately – and your father too if he's up and about!'

'No, the auld man's in bed,' said Willie, struggling wearily to his feet, stretching. 'What's the problem? Has he got a tight little hogg he canna lamb, is that it?'

'Nothing to do with sheep,' insisted Lucy, 'Much more desperate than that. . . . There's a robbery going on in the village – *NOW*!' She almost screamed the last word, and Willie was suddenly shaken wide awake.

Lucy gave him the picture on the journey back along the bottom road. She was in a sort of dramatic East European espionage mode now, driving at break-neck speed (often in the ditch – sidelights only). She was Olga the beautiful Bulgarian spy, racing to save the civilised world . . . dashing 007 (Willie) by her side. Together they would thwart the KGB, the Mafia, the Colombian drug cartel, whoever. . . . The fiendish villains now violating sleepy innocent Hindburn would be outwitted – shown no mercy . . .!

By the time the pick-up slid sideways into Geordie's yard, Willie was very pleased to get out. Geordie was waiting for them at the back door.

In the kitchen, Geordie's missus had stoked up the fire, brewed a pot of tea, and was kneeling on the cleaky mat attending to the nourishment of the feeble lamb from the cardboard box. She was gently pressing his adam's apple, making him swallow, persuading him to suck . . . murmuring encouragement. She seemed oblivious of the drama unfolding about her. The well-being of the lamb – far more important.

Willie took a mug from the scrubbed table. 'So are y' absolutely sure about this invasion?' he asked. He wanted to hear Geordie's side of the story. He wasn't entirely convinced by Lucy's excitable report. These eccentric women from south of the Tyne weren't always totally reliable. She might've been on the gin all night for all he knew.

'Oh I think it's right enough,' Geordie said, his back to the fire, rubbing the backs of his legs. 'There's definitely two strange vans up by the Hart. I've seen them creepin' about m'self earlier on.'

'How many blokes?' Willie wanted to know.

'Anybody's guess,' Geordie shrugged. 'Maybe half a dozen – canna tell, but they'll be proper hooligans for sure. If they're doin' the Post Office, they might even be armed!'

There was a tap on the door, and Tommy Cleghorn came in. Doreen noticed he didn't take his wellies off, but said nowt. Just gave him a withering look.

'They're still there,' Tommy whispered, as if the thieves were just outside the door. He'd crept up through the croft behind 'The Forge' to have a look for himself, while Lucy was fetching Willie. 'And what's more,' he said, pausing for the right effect . . . 'I reckon one of them has a gun. Couldn't be absolutely sure, too dark . . . but y' know how somebody would carry a shotgun – well I'm pretty sure he had a gun. He was a big bugger too!'

'Jesus,' Willie exclaimed. 'We're not gonna have a battle in the middle of Hindburn, are we? Somebody could get hurt here!'

'I've got a .22,' Tommy said, 'and you farmers always have a shotgun hidden away somewhere. We could get Sep out of bed as well!'

All this time Lucy had been missing. Only now did they realise she hadn't come into the house with Willie. Nobody had noticed her absence until she came back breathless. 'They've been everywhere!' she gasped. 'I've just found the Grahams locked in a cupboard, but I can't get them out. It'll take two men to shift the furniture. . . . The vicarage is stripped bare. They're in an awful state . . . I told them to hang on and I'd get some help. I think she's having a breakdown . . .!'

'Just leave them where they are,' said Geordie quietly. 'The last thing we need is a distressed woman running up and down the village, howlin'.'

They were all looking at the man in disbelief. Lucy was about to protest at his callous heartless chauvinist attitude, but he held up his hand to stop her. It was a very big hand. 'Another twenty minutes won't do them any harm,' he said . . . 'and we don't really want to disturb the

thieves, do we? I mean we don't want them to run away
. . . not yet.'

'What y' on about?' Tommy asked.

Geordie had moved away from the fire, his bum nicely
warmed now. 'Well look at it this way,' he said. 'We can't
get the police here until we find a phone that works, can
we? They must've cut the wires. And even if we did find
one, maybe up at Hindhope, or somewhere beyond that . . .
by the time the constabulary gets here, those buggers will
probably be long gone . . . finished. I bet they're plannin' to
clean up and be away by four o'clock at the latest . . . before
there's any light, before folks start gettin' up to let the dog
out . . . before the milkman delivers. . . . Once they're gone,
they're gone!' said Geordie firmly. 'You'll never see *them* or
the loot again. Not once they get into Newcastle. They'll
just disappear!'

'So what do we do?' Lucy asked. 'It's nearly three
o'clock!'

'Right,' said Geordie, just the merest suspicion of a grin
on his face. 'Tommy, I want you to make sure those vans
stay where they are for a while.'

'Me?' said Tommy. 'They'll shoot me!'

'Rubbish – they'll never see you, y' sneaky little divil.
You're always creepin' about at night poachin'. You know
every rock and rabbit hole for miles. I don't care how y' do
it, but wherever those vehicles are – cripple them. Let the
tyres down, pinch the keys, pull a few wires out . . . anythin' y' like, but give them somethin' to worry about. And
don't get caught!'

'Now?' Tommy asked.

'The sooner the better,' said Geordie. 'On yer way!'

Tommy zipped up his jacket, wiped his nose on the back
of his hand, and vanished into the night.

'Lucy darlin',' said Geordie (he was beginning to enjoy

this). 'Give us twenty minutes, then start checkin' on anybody else who might be locked in a cupboard. . . .' He was halfway to the door. 'Willie,' he beckoned. 'Come wi' me. . . . We haven't much time!'

Obviously, Geordie had a plan.

CHAPTER SIXTEEN

Getting into the little Post Office was not too difficult. Any fool could smash their way in, grab a handful of fivers, and scarper. The trick was to do it without creating a major disturbance . . . so far this exercise had gone very sweetly. Gazza didn't want any cock-ups now.

Kev soon sussed out the alarm system. There was a bright red alarm box high on the wall above the front door – but that was only an empty deterrent. The real thing sat hidden away among the ivy on the gable end . . . the wires running back through the wall into the loft. You couldn't get at them to snip and disconnect. It would take the expanding foam filler to choke the thing to death. There was possibly a BT link to the police as well, but that was hopefully taken care of already. The two double sensors linked to lights front and side presented no real difficulty either. The best ploy was to sneak up underneath and cover the eye with sticky black tape. The lights wouldn't respond after that. If for some unconsidered reason they persisted in shining, Kev would promptly smash the bulbs with a stick. Not a very sophisticated technique perhaps, and rather too noisy – but it would quickly restore covering darkness.

Gazza was out of the van quietly directing operations. Kev halfway up a ladder with his foam gun at the ready. Sol on the flat garage roof waiting to go through the landing window.

One thing you could say about Sol, he generally did as he was told. Nothing subtle or devious about the lad. Not stupid you understand, but somewhat naive, childlike even sometimes. However as far as Gazza was concerned, he was totally 'biddable'. Consequently when Gazza told Sol to break the window, he did so . . . just before Gazza could add, 'When I give you the nod.'

'When I give you the nod,' was drowned first by the splintering crash as Sol violently kicked in the whole window frame and leapt through onto the stairs . . . and secondly by the bell that Kev hadn't quite disabled yet. The embarrassing noise was over in seconds, but it was very disturbing.

Wally leaning on the van over in the pub car park heard it and ducked nervously out of sight. Kev silently prayed the foam would hurry up and suffocate the jangling racket . . . three . . . four . . . five . . . and it did. Peace again. Gazza muttered something obscene and waited anxiously by the transit. No new lights came on in the village, no troublesome dogs began to bark. Nobody seemed to be bothered. Lucky.

Inside, Sol switched on his pencil torch, holding it with his left hand along the barrel of the gun, pointed ahead at hip level. The safety catch was on. Gazza had told him to keep it 'on' at all times. Disappointing – but at least he felt like the real thing. No more pussyfooting about. He was the guy with the artillery. Nobody would push *him* around. Barclays Bank, Fort Knox, village Post Office . . . it didn't matter.

He smashed in the first door he came to. He could easily have opened it by turning the knob – but it seemed 'tougher' this way. The bathroom was empty. Sol was about to push his foot through the next door along the landing, his boot already on its way, when the door opened. Sol went through into the room like a rampant rhinoceros. There was no resistance to slow him down . . . and he ended up in a confused heap at the foot of the bed.

Fred, visibly shaken, switched on the light, and stood there in his wee Willie Winky nightshirt, still holding the door handle. Doris sitting up clutching Fred's pillow as if it might be bulletproof.

'Put that bloody light out!' Sol snarled, on his feet now, in control again, the gun pointing straight at Fred's belly. Fred readily did as he was told, and put his hands in the air.

'Get outa bed!' Sol growled at Doris, and the terrified lady scrambled from her warm refuge, still hanging onto the pillow, very eager not to upset the monster. She'd never seen anyone so huge.

'Downstairs, no lights, no trouble.' The orders came out the side of Sol's mouth – like in one of those old black-and-white movies he'd seen on a wet Sunday afternoon . . . Bogart and Cagney thumping everybody. Sol certainly wasn't about to tolerate any nonsense from a couple of old 'crumblies' like these. Not with a 'piece' in his hand. He poked the barrel sharply into Fred's back as he and Doris shuffled out of the room and past the broken window. Intimidation was hardly necessary – they weren't going to turn and attack the great hulk . . . but he wanted them to know just who was in charge. The boss would be really

134

impressed with his attitude.

'Y' muckle daft bugger, you nearly made a proper balls of that, didn't y'?' Gazza hissed at him, as the door was unbolted and Sol let his comrades in.

Gazza didn't appear to be happy at all. He grabbed Fred by the front of his shirt and almost shouted right into his face – spittle coming through the hole in the black balaclava. Terrifying. 'This big thick mate of mine is very likely to shoot you *and* your wife if we have any bother. Understood?'

Fred nodded vigorously. Doris clung to his arm beginning to sob. She couldn't help it. She was finding it difficult to breathe. 'He's a bloody maniac!' snarled Gazza. . . . 'Nothin' he likes better than hurtin' people. It's his job, he loves it!' Sol was grinning, flicking the safety catch on and off, looking even bigger than usual in the torch light.

Kev had already emptied the till and was breaking open locked drawers. Stuffing money into a white canvas holdall. Gazza was poking a finger into Fred's chest. 'I want every penny you've got,' he said. He spat it out slowly and deliberately.

Later, when it was all over, after the police had fingerprinted the shop, when the man from the *Chronicle* came to get the story, and the locals dropped by to commiserate, and hear the gory details first hand, Doris told them all, 'We're lucky to be alive. They were like animals,' she said. 'I've never been so frightened in my life!'

'Did they beat you?' the reporter asked. 'Did they abuse you in any way?' He was looking for a dramatic headline, a juicy angle . . . blood on the front page.

'Fred'll never be the same again,' said Doris. 'We're retiring at the end of the year, selling up. It's just not worth it.'

However she had to admit the gang had never actually hit

135

them. Oh yes, they'd pushed and shoved and shouted. . . .
The big one had waved his gun about, and in the end they'd
been tied up and gagged with a roll of sticky tape, and left in
the kitchen till Tommy Cleghorn found them there. It had
been a terrible ordeal. They'd have nightmares for the rest of
their lives. But no, nobody had beaten them over the head.

The man from the *Chronicle* was quite disappointed.

In fact it hadn't been necessary. Fred was very disinclined to
be a hero, and told them whatever they wanted to know.
What else could he do? He opened up the Post Office
counter and watched them fill the bag. Doris could barely
speak, let alone scream for help. The gang were in and out
in less than half an hour. Gazza estimated they must've
cleared well over five grand. A lot more when the stamps
and giros and postal orders were cashed.

*   *   *

The White Hart was a cushy number too. No interference.

Sol, still attached to the sawn-off twelve bore, was left to
guard the blue VW at the shop, while just over the road
Gazza and Kev joined Wally to 'do' the pub. The boss
waited outside, having a quiet smoke as the two smaller
men climbed in through a conveniently open window. It
led directly into the bar area, shrouded in darkness, the
odour of fags and beer and customers still lingering in the
air. Within minutes they were handing cash, cigarettes and
spirits out through the window . . . Gazza pushing these
into whatever space was available in the BT van. It was
loaded to the roof now, sitting well down on the springs.
Heavy. It was almost time to creep quietly out of this dozy
little hole and head back home. There was an empty lock-
up garage waiting for them, Kev had the keys.

Gazza called a halt just after half-past three. Okay, that
would do. It had been a canny night's work. All he wanted
now was a couple of good motors to complete the job. The

136

Jag and the Merc would be the icing on the cake. He would drive the Jag home himself. Yes sir, even the big boys would talk about this little caper for years to come. It would become a piece of low-life folklore. They'd tell their bairns about it. The story would get blown up of course, until it became the night Gazza's amazing gang 'cleaned out' a whole town in one night. It would be positively inspiring.

They found it hard not to giggle and snigger, it had been so easy. 'It's all down to the planning,' said Gazza modestly.

* * *

Kev and Wally were dispatched to the Peabody's front drive to quietly relieve him of the gleaming 4-litre XJS. Kev reckoned he could get it moving within a couple of minutes. He was a 'pro'. No motor had beaten him yet.

'Right, we'll meet you at the big house at the end of the village,' said Gazza. 'What's it called? – Haugh House . . . then you can start the Merc, and we'll be on our way. Ten minutes maximum. Home for breakfast eh?'

The first indication that this schedule might be a bit optimistic came with the deafening blast of Sol's gun.

Gazza was driving the BT truck gently out of the pub car park, still no lights, turning right in front of the Post Office, winding down the window to tell Sol to follow when . . . Boom! The crazy bugger was waking the dead! Then the second barrel went off. 'Jesus, what y' doin'?' Gazza yelled, 'Come on!'

'I saw somebody,' Sol protested. 'He was right there behind the van, honest!'

Gazza was suddenly nervous. 'Forget it,' he shouted, 'Let's go!'

'I saw 'im,' Sol insisted. 'He was fiddlin' about at the back. . . .'

'Fetch the bloody van,' screamed Gazza, 'For God's sake stop pissin' about!'

137

He waited just long enough for Sol to climb into the cab, start the engine, and begin to ease out into the road. Again he fully expected the entire village to suddenly light up . . . irate peasants appearing in the street loading old sporting guns, sharpening pitchforks. But surprisingly only one light came on − at 'The Forge'. Maybe guns going off in the dead of night were a common occurrence in these parts. Poachers? Bird scarers? Who knows?

He was very relieved to see the Jag come past (no doubt about it, Kev was good). It pulled up outside Haugh House garden gate, as Gazza glanced back to see Sol's blue van in the rear-view mirror. They were still on course, but no time to lose now. He pulled onto the verge behind the XJS, waving Sol to do the same.

'Any trouble at the other end of the village?' Gazza asked as Kev got out of the car. 'This silly sod started shootin' at ghosts when you were down there. I thought he might've disturbed the natives. . . .'

'No,' said Kev. 'Some activity at the farm maybe, but there's been lights on there all night. Nothing else that we could see.'

'The VW's not goin' very well,' said Sol, 'Rattlin' and thumpin' like a bag o' hammers.'

'You've got a flat.' Wally had heard the rhythmical bump bump bump as it came up the road, and had gone to take a look. 'In fact you've got two,' he said. . . . 'Both back wheels.'

'I *knew* there was somebody there,' Sol exclaimed. 'So *that's* what he was doin' − I hope I shot 'im!'

'Could we use the spares, like from both vans?' suggested Wally . . . then quickly dismissed the idea. 'No, the transit wheel wouldn't fit, would it?'

Kev had opened the boot lid on the Jaguar, just to see what extra bonus there might be in there. He found a set of golf clubs (wondered briefly what they were worth), the car's tool kit and a foot pump. 'Will they blow up?' he asked, 'or has he slashed them?'

'Doesn't matter,' said Wally, down on his knees inspecting the damage. 'The tyres are nearly shredded anyway. The van's way overloaded y' know. It'll be a helluva weight like!'

Gazza was becoming more and more agitated now. There wasn't time to stand about discussing flat tyres. 'Well we're not leavin' it here,' he growled. 'We'll take it home on the *rims* if we have to . . . it's only twenty-five miles. And if that doesn't work, we'll just have t' hide it somewhere, and come back later . . . transfer the load. . . .'

He held the door open. 'Wally, you drive the thing, and take it easy. . . .' He didn't want Sol behind the wheel, certainly not on his own. That silly prat would probably shoot the vehicle to death, if it conked out on him.

'In fact maybe you should set off now,' said Gazza. 'Get a bit of a start . . . we'll follow in a minute.'

As Wally got in, turned the ignition and began to wobble slowly up the lane towards Hindhope, Kev went to nick the Merc. The big double garage was stuck onto the back of the house, probably with a connecting door into the kitchen area – so that these high society folk never got their posh frocks wet, or mud on their Gucci shoes.

Climbing onto Sol's massive shoulders, he broke the small frosted glass panel high up on the side wall, removed the splinters, and with a struggle squeezed through feet first. Halfway in, he twisted round, clung onto the window frame, and dropped into the darkness. Kev found the light switch easily enough, but thought better of it. Instead he pressed the button that would open the doors, and watched as the electric motor buzzed, and pushed the heavy flexidoor up into the roof. In the dingy light he could make out the spotless white 500 SL with GB plates, and standing next to it, Polly's red Polo. He wasn't interested in that. The little sister could stay where she was – it was the big flashy brother Kev wanted.

Gazza and Sol were waiting outside for his signal. 'You can go,' he said quietly, 'I'll be right behind you.'

Gazza ran to the Jag, and Sol heaved himself into the transit, both vehicles parked on the roadside, ready for the getaway. Kev watched them move off, and turned to deal with the car. It shouldn't be too difficult. He was looking forward to driving this machine. Maybe he'd go back a different way, take his time, listen to the stereo, relax in the leather seats. Might even open it up along the Western Bypass, see what it could do . . . 150 mph they reckoned. It would fetch a very good price.

He was only mildly surprised to find the car unlocked with the keys hanging in the ignition. Some people imagined they were safe in a garage. . . . Oh yeah? Naturally it started at the first turn. Kev inhaled the lovely expensive smell, dug out a bent Benson and Hedges from a crumpled packet in his boiler suit, and waited for the lighter to pop out. The radio offered hits from the sixties. That would do for the time being. He pushed the lever into drive and eased the car gently out towards the road. Only the gravel under the wheels making any significant noise.

The lads had gone right. They would head due west as arranged, take the B roads through Stamfordham and sneak into the city by Wylam. That's if Wally's van survived the course. If the worst came to the worst, they would dump the 'lame' beast somewhere out of sight, empty the transit, and go back for the other load. They might've transferred some of the smaller stuff into the Jag already. Anyway, it had nothing to do with him – that was Gazza's problem. Well, let's face it, Kev had done more than his fair share this night.

He turned left out of Haugh House, back towards the village and the A1. He wondered if there were yet more golf clubs in the boot of *this* car. He'd find out soon enough.

CHAPTER SEVENTEEN

It all happened so quickly. For some of the bit players, in this drama, it *had* to.

For Tommy Cleghorn it was one of the dodgiest nights he could remember. Since Linda's dad found them both in an agitated condition among the bales in Geordie's hayshed, years ago. Since the Colonel caught him setting snares in Marley wood.

Tonight, he couldn't get anywhere near the van at the White Hart. There was always somebody there keeping a look-out, and he didn't know how dangerous the man might be. Did he have a gun? Perhaps there were others inside the pub. Who could tell? They might appear at any time. Over at the Post Office he'd already seen at least three blokes, and he was fairly sure one of *them* was armed. No, this wasn't just a couple of spotty teenage joyriders out to pinch a car on a quiet night. We were talking professional villains here. The job had probably been planned for weeks. If they caught a glimpse of Tommy, they were hardly likely to drop everything and just run away. They'd beat the yoghurt out of 'im! Whatever happened, he had to stay out of sight.

Creeping about like a nervous rabbit, ears pricked, hopping and squatting under the hedge that separated Mr Pratt's little field from the shop, he'd managed to get quite close to the action. He was half frozen, wet knees, cold hands . . . he dare not cough, a potential sneeze had to be stifled. He'd almost given up hope of ever doing any damage to either van when it happened. The CRASH! The breaking glass . . . the bell . . . not for long, but a real commotion while it lasted. Maybe they'd blown it. They might be forced to abandon the robbery altogether, and flee before he could do anything sensational to delay them.

Tommy peered cautiously through into Fred and Doris's back garden. It had gone quiet again. No sign of the thieves, but the blue VW was still there. Perhaps this was his last chance.

Gently, quietly, he squeezed through between the railings, and scrambled on all fours the fifteen or twenty yards to the rear of the van. So far so good. . . . He considered simply stabbing the tyres, but wasn't sure what sort of noise that would make. They might explode. If he went to the cab and opened the door, chances were a light would come on. The last thing he wanted was a confrontation with these characters. Tommy didn't fancy being mutilated for the sake of a few postage stamps. He didn't need a medal . . . and certainly not posthumously!

He pressed a valve with the point of his pocket knife, and was dismayed at the horrendous hissing noise that ensued. It probably wasn't very loud really, but to him it sounded as if it was being attacked by a whole army of vipers . . . twice. It was all over in less than a minute, but not a minute too soon. He just had time to roll under the vehicle as three men came out of the shop carrying bags. From his hiding place he could see six feet as the men loaded their loot through the rear doors. Then four feet left, leaving one pair of enormous brown boots visible at the front end. Dammit – he was trapped there with a giant gangster no more than three yards away.

Tommy lay still for what seemed like a decade. Maybe they would eventually drive off and never notice him . . . but that was doubtful. Somebody would surely see the flat tyres and come to investigate. Then his goose would be well and truly cooked, no mistake.

It was Gloria Swanson's tom cat who resolved the dilemma. Sol, already on edge, must have heard the moggy making his way home after a night on the tiles. A rustle of twigs and leaves as the cat jumped down from the fence. 'Who's that?' he shouted – and without waiting for an answer, or even taking aim at anything in particular, he spun round and fired – completely decimating a perfectly innocent forsythia.

Tommy thought he heard pellets hit the van, but was disinclined to linger and assess the damage. Scrambling blindly out from under the back number plate, he leapt to his feet, and ran as fast as he could. He wasn't trying to hide now. The only thing on his mind was to increase the range, and find total darkness. He stumbled down through the Post Office garden, cleared the fence like a hurdler, and hit the ground still running into the Marleyburn field . . . minus one wellie. Sol saw but a fleeting shadow somewhere beyond the van, and sent the second barrel in that general direction. Tommy heard the pellets peppering the fence, and somebody cursing. He didn't stop till he hobbled into the sanctuary of Geordie's shed . . . and only then realised his right buttock was tingling, rather like a very nasty nettle sting.

* * *

That first explosion probably woke Trevor Pratt. The second one certainly did. In any case it had been a restless night. He had a lot on his mind, a busy day tomorrow, figures fluttering about in his head. Sleep hadn't taken hold at all. He imagined he'd heard traffic and voices . . . just a general feeling of unease all night, but perhaps he'd been dreaming. Eventually he slid silently out of bed, watched Celia stretch and spread herself over onto his side – and went downstairs for a cup of tea.

The disaster didn't hit him immediately. When it *did* begin to register, he couldn't believe it . . . and stood staring open mouthed at the chaos for a full minute.

Amanda appeared at the kitchen doorway in pink pyjamas, bare feet. 'What's going on Daddy?' she asked . . . still half asleep, rubbing her eyes, fingers pushed through tousled hair – not really with it.

'We've been damn-well burgled!' Trevor shouted, sounding as if it was her fault. 'Can't you see the bloody mess?'

He began to wander slowly from room to room, picking his way among the debris . . . from kitchen to lounge to dining room, and finally into his office. The safe was gone, that was the first thing he noticed. His desk was a disaster area. They must have his credit cards. Judging from the sea of paper scattered on the floor, it would take days to reorganise client accounts. Some might be missing altogether, stuffed into a bag in the mad evil scramble for anything of value. He saw a calamity. He saw weeks of work down the drain. He saw trouble with his partners, the police, the insurance company . . . not to mention the rest of the family. He saw the dead telephone, the clean wall

145

where the microwave had stood, the bare TV trolley, the empty sideboard, the upturned drawers . . . the broken door in the utility room. He saw Butch dozing by the Aga, apparently unconcerned, his tail giving an occasional friendly twitch. 'Oh my God,' he groaned, and went to wake Celia.

Halfway up the stairs he met Amanda coming down three at a time – fully dressed now, wide awake. He watched her leap into the red wellies and dash out into the night. 'Where on earth are *you* going?' he yelled, too late. 'Come back at once!'

She was half way to the Glebe Farm by then.

* * *

Lucy found Linda Cleghorn up and about, concerned where Tommy had got to. 'He usually leaves a note when he goes out at night,' she said. 'What's going on?'

Together they managed to move the big sideboard at the vicarage, just enough to release the wailing Grahams. Gordon was 'dying' of hypothermia and could barely speak – teeth chattering, head still aching from Gazza's blows . . . feet, hands and nose an unattractive blue. The first thing he did was cling to a radiator, and moan softly.

Shelagh ran all over the house upstairs and downstairs, back and forth, in and out of every room, waving her arms about, howling in anguish . . . hysterical. Gordon suspected the poor woman would need 'counselling'. In fact if she didn't shut up and settle down very soon, he might be forced to administer it himself. Once he'd been defrosted.

Lucy made them a pot of tea, and borrowing Linda's bike pedalled to the Hall. She had no idea what might have happened there, maybe nothing . . . but felt someone should check on her aristocratic friend. As she pedalled up the drive, she could see the front door was ajar, a thin beam of light coming out from the house, a rusty old sword lying on the top step. 'Who's there?' shouted a voice from inside. 'Stay where you are or I'll shoot!'

She found Miss Angela where the thieves had left her, strapped securely to the banisters at the foot of the stairs. The brave border terriers peering cautiously round the corner along the passage.

'Have they caught the barstards?' Miss Angela demanded. 'God I'm freezing, shut the damned door and get me a brandy!'

The old girl was stiff and cold, but none the worse for her ordeal. Tough as old boots. She rubbed her wrists and ankles where the rope marks showed red, and went to get dressed. 'We'll form a posse,' she growled, 'and hunt them down. No mercy, we'll hang the lot of them!'

* * *

At about the same time, Tommy Cleghorn (wearing one of Geordie's reserve pair), went to retrieve his wayward wellie from the field. He found several sheep viewing it with suspicion. By the time he reached the Post Office garden he was thankfully wearing his own and carrying the spare. He hoped he wouldn't have to explain this to anyone.

He came upon a very depressed Trevor Pratt sitting on the fence talking to his daughter's horse. Trevor wondered what this man was doing wandering about in the middle of the night with an odd wellie tucked under his arm, but didn't ask. It only confirmed an impression he'd had for some time, that country folk were a totally different breed, and a bit weird.

'We've been robbed,' he sobbed. 'The house has been turned upside down. I'm probably ruined . . . and the phones don't work . . .!'

'I know,' said Tommy. 'I mean I know you've been robbed . . . so has half the village.'

He groped his way through to the Post Office, by more

or less the same route he'd used when fleeing earlier. There was no sign of the van or the burglars. The front door of the shop was open, and with some trepidation he went in and switched on the light. At first sight the shop looked very much as it always did – groceries neatly stacked on shelves and display cabinets . . . but behind the counter it was obvious every drawer and cupboard had been rifled.

He found them in the kitchen, taped up and wild eyed, unable to make a sound, greatly relieved to see Tommy. When they first heard him coming, their worst fear was one of the gangsters (probably the big nasty one) had returned to finish them off. Well, as Doris said, 'Masks or no masks, we might have recognised them in an identity parade . . . and people like that don't usually leave live witnesses lying about, do they?'

Tommy suggested they maybe shouldn't try to tidy up until the police had been, but he suspected they would. Fred and Doris were tidy folk . . . everything in its place. They'd probably have the shop open at eight o'clock as normal.

Over the road he was forced to bang and shout at the pub to rouse Jack and Nora. They weren't exactly delighted to see him, he knew they wouldn't be. The news he brought wasn't good, but this was hardly an occasion to shoot the messenger. In any case Jack might well be needed before the night was out. He was a handy bloke to have on your side if it ever came to a punch-up. When the couple saw the damage in the bar, they were both quite capable of homicide. Foamin'.

* * *

Up on the hill at Hindhope, Freddie Fox QC was at the end of his tether. Earlier, sometime after midnight, he and his neighbours had set off bravely into the night to sabotage

148

Sep's bird scarer. Barry Beeday the plumber had insisted on taking his springer spaniel. 'Thatcher will sniff it out wherever it's hidden,' he boasted. 'She's a trial dog y' know.'

At the first explosion, Thatcher had quickly gone home, retired . . . but at least the men now had a rough idea where the weapon was deployed. 'Somewhere over there!' declared Foxie, pointing to the trees on the far side of the rape field.

At the second explosion, fifteen minutes later, they realised it was now behind them, they'd gone too far. It was dark, their designer wellies had picked up a ton of clarts, it was cold and drizzly. They waited, but the banger missed the next few 'beats' altogether. It didn't fire. Undoubtedly it would 'click', but they heard nothing. They'd been plodging about in a field for nearly an hour, while the fiendish unreliable gun seemed determined to make fools of them. Sometimes it went off, sometimes it didn't. This was taking much longer than anticipated. Chances are they would never have found it in the dark anyway. Sep had it concealed in the wood, so the noise would echo and reverberate and ricochet around the trees, multiplying the effect . . . keeping the pigeons puzzled as well. He hoped he'd persuade the greedy fat pests to go and eat Charlie Harrison's rape instead. Nothing personal y' understand . . . anybody else's crop would do nicely.

Eventually the Hindhope quartet had given up the challenge. The plumber was seriously concerned about his dog, Gaskett the car dealer feared he was suffering from exposure, and Gerald from the Old Farmhouse felt he was on the brink of a cardiac. Foxie called the expedition off at a quarter to two. They were all totally exhausted. The banger resumed regular firing as soon as they reached the shelter of their exclusive executive homes.

149

The QC had then inserted ear plugs and wrapped himself in a duvet, and had been attempting to grab some sleep in an armchair when the tractor traffic began about two hours later. It was roaring up and down the road from Clartiehole, and turning at the top of the lonnen . . . right outside his house!

Enough! This was definitely too much! He tried the phone in the kitchen again. Still dead. Apoplectic with rage he stormed outside to his BMW and grabbed the car phone. Why hadn't he thought of it earlier? Perhaps he hadn't been quite so desperate then. Maybe it had barely been a police matter. He didn't really want to involve them in a civil war with the natives. But ye gods, this had been going on all night! Now, if he could, he'd be happy to call in the SAS to annihilate the whole lot of them. A temperamental bird scarer was bad enough, but revolting peasants ploughing or muck spreading (or whatever they were up to) at quarter to four in the morning was absolutely ridiculous! 'I know they get up early,' he told the duty sergeant, 'but this is past a bloody joke!'

The sergeant promised to send someone over as soon as possible . . . well, let's face it, the QC was a very influential man. Tonight he was being a pompous nuisance, making a fuss about nowt probably . . . but better to keep on the right side of folk like Foxie.

PC Percival and WPC Prendergast were despatched in the Escort van.

* * *

There was considerable activity down below the Glebe Farm as well. No bird scarers here, but certainly voices and a tractor growling in the dark, like some noisy nocturnal predator. Diana Peabody at Paddock House heard it all. After the row with Donald about 'the bloody awful good life', she hadn't slept well. It wasn't that she regretted her outburst, far from it. On the contrary she was still furious, more convinced than ever that this rural idyll was not for her. At least not all day and every day. . . . There would have to be changes.

Eventually she got out of bed and went downstairs to raid the fridge (she always ate when angry). The noise outside was puzzling, especially at this hour. Perhaps someone was stealing their ghastly animals . . . rustlers eh? Excellent. Let the fools get on with it. In fact she might even go out and help them.

Diana donned boots and jacket, and munching goat cheese on a wholemeal crust, picked up the torch and went out into the early morning. In the paddock behind the house the 'flock' was lying by the troughs, ready to pounce on her at the next feed. 'Your days are numbered,' she muttered under her breath, and moved round into the driveway. Out on the road, the big blue Ford tractor from Glebe Farm went roaring past – one of those monster bales stuck on the spiky thing at the front.

What on earth was Mr Dodds doing at this Godforsaken hour? She realised the lambing was a twenty-four hours a day job – but this was nonsense. She would have to wave the man down and tell him so. She was certainly in the right mood for a confrontation. These feudal farmers thought they could get away with anything. . . .

The tractor was manoeuvring somewhere beyond the War Memorial. She heard it rev and turn, and stepped out into the road waving her flashlight. Geordie braked when he saw her, opened the cab door, and before the lady could begin her hurriedly prepared protestations, he said, 'So have you been done as well then?'

'What?' Diana spluttered, somewhat deflated.

'Have y' been robbed, burgled?' asked Geordie. 'Everybody else has, and the villains are still here I think. . . .'

'Burgled? No, well I don't think so.' Diana was floundering a bit. 'What are you talking about. . .?'

'There's a gang o' tearaways cleanin' out the whole village,' said Geordie. Diana thought he seemed remarkably dispassionate about it. 'Where's your husband's fancy car?' he asked.

CHAPTER EIGHTEEN

Kev drove the Merc slowly through the village on dipped headlights. No need for a seat belt, just stretch out and listen to the 5-litre V8 engine purring softly. The Beatles were singing 'Hey Jude' on the radio, the air conditioning blowing cool. Once out of this sleepy (sparrow fart) hamlet, he'd open it up . . . glide into town, and meet up with the boys. It had been a piece of cake. Maybe they'd do it again some night. The countryside must be full of quaint old villages transformed into rich commuter communes now . . . full o' money . . . easy . . . 'Hey Jude, don't let me down . . . take a sad song and make it b-e-etter. . . .'

Jesus! He almost ran straight into it. What the hell was this? Kev stood on the brakes, and switched to full beam. Ahead of him the road was completely blocked! Hedge to hedge, no gaps. A twelve foot wall of . . . what was it? Straw or hay? Who cared? Solid – a ruddy great barricade of round bales three high, and God knows how many deep. No way through. *No way through*! And worse . . . somebody sitting on top holding a shotgun in his lap . . . grinning.

Geordie gave him a cheeky little wave as Kev whipped his machine into reverse, and screamed backwards to the farmyard entrance. He bounced off a stone gatepost, spun round . . . and accelerated back up the village street the way he'd come. The car was going much quicker now. The noise didn't matter anymore, the lights were of no consequence. The Beatles silenced, suddenly an annoyance. He couldn't concentrate with the fab four twittering on about Eleanor Rigby. He had plenty of problems of his own without worrying about her. He had to get out of here, quickly! Past the Post Office and the pub (signs of life there already). Down over the wee bridge that spanned the burn. . . . Past Haugh House where he'd so recently acquired this motor, and westwards up the hill towards Hindhope and freedom . . . the way the rest of the gang had gone. He should've just followed them. He'd soon catch up. This Merc was a really quick machine. He'd crested the hill, changed into fourth . . . going about seventy – when he saw the bright red tail lights only fifty yards ahead.

Gazza had got there first in the Jag. He'd been rolling along congratulating himself, luxuriating in the brown leather upholstery, fidgeting with the CD player. The VW hobbling twenty yards behind on its solid back wheels – the transit and Wally bringing up the rear of the convoy . . . Kev and his Merc due any minute . . . when there it was! Would you believe it? A monster green tractor with gigantic wheels, connected to another enormous piece of agricultural gear, like a huge red barrel on wheels – parked right across the bloody road! There was a bloke in the cab, just sitting there. Smoking a fag! What the hell was he playing at? Was he stuck, broken down? Was he drunk? Had he jack-knifed? Was he mad? Was he turning into a field? There was no bleedin' gate!

Then it dawned on him. This was not some conscientious peasant up with the larks, making an early start to the day, no sir. It wasn't a silly wayward yokel who'd taken the wrong turning either. This was a 'No through road' sign. An agricultural road block!

Even more discouraging was yet another big bright tractor standing just beyond, with a massive metal bucket scoop attached to its front end, sticking up in the air. Inside this elevated vantage point Gazza could clearly see a stocky figure sitting on the rim holding a torch. And was that a gun lying over his knees, perhaps?

Willie raised one hand. 'Good morning lads,' he shouted.

Gazza didn't hang about to exchange pleasantries. He got the picture. He leapt out of the car and waving his arms at Sol and Wally, he yelled, 'Back the other way! They've got us cut off here. Turn around!'

There wasn't a lot of room on the narrow country road for a quick about-face, and all three vehicles had completed no more than three of their five-point turns (Sol having serious difficulties with his damaged van) when Kev came over the brow like a tornado. He hit Wally's VW smack bang amidships . . . moving it and the unfortunate Wally several yards sideways into the dyke. The Merc careered off into a tree on the other side of the road. The car's front end a mangled mess, steam and smoke rising from the wreckage. The boot lid had flown open on impact, and Kev had continued on through the windscreen into the ditch. He now lay there groaning, holding his bleeding head, while Sol and Gazza ran to drag a shaky Wally from his buckled cab. None of them had noticed the body of Giles Pollock lying with his little bag in the boot of the Merc, a neat hole in the back of his skull.

* * *

Gazza surveyed the remnants of his army. Half the transport was completely written off. Two of his men wounded, one of them quite seriously perhaps. Only the Jag and an over-loaded transit operational. The road blocked with heavy equipment, the peasants at the barricade. This was really serious. He quickly decided a strategic withdrawal was the only sensible course of action.

'All the cash into the car,' he ordered. 'Quickly, leave the other stuff . . . c'mon let's go!'

Sol began transferring holdalls and bags from both vans, Wally doing his best to help, limping badly. All the money, jewellery and smaller precious items they'd nicked throughout the night were packed into the boot and onto the back seats. It would still be a useful haul.

Gazza went to pull Kev from the gutter. 'Don't worry,' he said, easing him gently up onto the bank, 'You'll be alright, we're going back now, we'll just take the Jag . . . make a run for it, head the other way onto the A1. We'll be home in half an hour. . . .'

'I doubt it,' Kevin groaned miserably. 'There's another road block down by the farm. You'll not get out that way. They've got stuff stacked a mile high! We're knackered mate . . . trapped!'

'We could shoot our way out,' said Sol. 'I've still got two shells left.'

'Please yerself,' said Gazza, 'but that bloke up in the bucket would have you first I reckon. . . . You're on yer own.'

'Okay, we could make a run for it,' Sol persisted. 'Y' know – take off over the fields, get lost in the dark. . . .'

'For God's sake shut up,' snapped Gazza. 'Kev and Wally

156

canna run anywhere . . . and it'll be light soon, we wouldn't last five minutes.'

He leaned on the bonnet of the Jag. 'Let me think . . .' He suspected no one else would. 'There's only one thing for it,' he said. 'We'll have to negotiate.'

Sol wasn't very sure what that meant, but if Gazza thought it was an alternative escape route, he was all for it.

'Fetch the holdall with the money,' said Gazza. 'We'll go and talk to them, make them an offer . . .'

'You're like gonna buy our way out?' Wally asked.

'Everybody has a price,' Gazza smiled. 'Even farmers!'

The three desperados lined up and advanced slowly towards the blockade. Gazza had the bag in one hand, the other held high above his head. Sol on one side still carrying the gun, Wally on the other, hobbling and holding his right knee. They came within five or six yards of the machinery, before Willie up in the grain bucket said firmly, 'That's far enough.' He had his Pape twelve bore pointed directly at Sol's chest. It was an easy target. He wouldn't miss from this range. 'And tell that fat bloke to drop his little toy gun,' he snarled.

'Go on, put it down,' said Gazza quietly, and waited as Sol slowly, reluctantly obeyed . . . looking like a petulant laddie who's had his football taken away.

'We've got ten grand in here,' Gazza shouted, raising the holdall. 'It's yours if you move this machinery and let us through with the car. Everything else is in the two vans. We'll leave it. No harm done eh? Everybody gets their stuff back . . . we go home, and you get rich. What y' say?'

They saw the man in the John Deere cab turn round and look up towards the bucket, waiting for instructions. 'No, I don't think so,' said Willie from on high. 'I've got a better idea than that!'

They saw him nod to his father in the big green tractor.

They heard it start, heard the mounting revs . . . wondered for a moment if the man was about to move away. But no – Sep gently eased the drive-shaft into gear, and turned to watch through the window, as the rotary spreader began to hurl its stinking load of slurry towards the astonished outlaws. It was a shit storm! There was no time to escape. Within seconds they were covered from head to foot, blinded, in a foul-smelling torrent of manure. It flew into their eyes and soaked through their balaclavas. They turned their backs and felt it running down their necks. They ran, but the awful weapon had a substantial range, and they slipped and fell and floundered in the filthy stuff. Gazza desperately sought refuge sideways into the ditch . . . crawling along until he found a hole in the hedge – and squeezed through to the sanctuary of a field and darkness.

Wally simply couldn't stand up, and finally just lay down almost totally submerged in the gunge, resigned to the conclusion he must have arrived in hell.

Sol managed to stagger from the deluge, only to be met by Willie and two bewildered constables, who had arrived at the scene just as the terrible bombardment commenced. The four residents of Hindhope, weary after their futile search for the banger, looked on from the other side of the fence in total disbelief.

CHAPTER NINETEEN

By daylight on Tuesday morning, Freddie Fox QC was threatening legal action against Sep . . . charging him with seriously disturbing the peace, conspiring with others to unlawfully block the B6343, and wantonly depositing unsavoury substances on the highway, likely to pollute the environment and create a hazard.

In the village, police cars were everywhere, and a British Telecom crew were down in a hole by the churchyard, reconnecting wires. The breathless press were held at bay, while the *true* story of the great Hindburn robbery was unravelled.

Everybody in the village was interviewed. Notes were taken, lists compiled and checked off against the contents of the two vans and the Jag. The Merc was dragged away by 'forensic'.

Social Services, concerned that the trauma might have

proved too much for a little old lady living alone, quickly despatched an experienced team of stress counsellors to the Hall. Miss Angela Fenwicke-Browne met them at the front door and told them to 'bugger orf', before being whisked away by her friend Lucy, to join the queue of other victims retrieving their stolen property. Lucy was already composing an epic poem provisionally entitled 'The Rape of Hindburn'.

Gordon and Shelagh Graham were already making arrangements to vacate the old vicarage. 'We simply can't take anymore of this place,' said Shelagh. 'Gordon is a broken man . . . I think he might have just survived the ordeal, if the thieves had stolen the church clock – but it was not to be. . . .'

Fred and Doris Little opened their shop as usual at 8.00 am precisely. By then the only items unaccounted for appeared to be a white holdall containing a substantial amount of cash . . . and one Garry (Gazza) Gallacher (23) of no fixed address.

It took about an hour for the really big news to break. There was a corpse! Suddenly the great Hindburn robbery became the great Hindburn *murder* mystery. Inspector Moffatt, in charge of the case, would only confirm that the body of Giles Heathcote Pollock (56), a local businessman, had been recovered from the boot of his own car. Privately the Inspector considered it very unlikely that the victim had climbed in there, shot himself in the back of the head, disposed of the gun and closed the lid.

The three men already in custody were to be charged with aggravated burglary, but not (as yet) with the death of Mr Pollock. The Inspector went on to say his officers were anxious to interview a fourth man, whom they believed might help them with their enquiries. A description of Gazza was being circulated.

Extra police were drafted in and, together with a few local men, they combed the woods and hedgerows for the fugitive. Within an hour of the muck spreading incident, *official* road blocks were set up, and all vehicles within a ten-mile radius stopped and searched.

Gazza could see them from his hiding place among the bracken on the edge of Marley wood. He was cold, stinking, hungry and very miserable. Three hours now since he'd escaped from the farmers' fusillade of muck, crawled through the hedge and scrambled away into the dark. He had no idea how far he'd travelled – probably not very far . . . maybe round in circles for all he knew. Sometimes on his hands and knees, sometimes running, crouching, falling, stumbling in the gloom over wet clarty fields . . . until eventually, knackered, he'd found this refuge under the trees.

How the hell had he got into this mess? Dammit, it had so nearly been brilliant. If they'd left twenty minutes earlier they would've made it for sure. Poor Kev . . . at least he'd be in a warm hospital by now. The other two probably in the nick. Gazza wrapped his arms tight around the holdall. He wasn't done for yet.

No one from Hindburn went off to work that day. As well as making themselves available for questioning, those who had escaped the carnage naturally wanted to hear all the sordid details first hand. None of the village children attended school either, and Amanda, having checked her wardrobe and cassette collection were intact, spent the entire day with her shepherding guru.

Geordie was back in his lambing shed as soon as he and Tommy had removed the bales from the highway. In his absence, two pairs and a single had been born with no apparent difficulty. However a mother of triplets, presumably exhausted by her efforts, had sat on one of her brood, and smothered the poor creature t' death. All things considered a canny night's work. A long one though. He was tired. Thank God for his 'bonnie wee apprentice'. She would be a big help until he got his wind back.

Sep drove into the yard soon after ten-thirty – just as Geordie, D'reen baby and Tommy Cleghorn were about to have a cup of tea. 'They got 'im,' Sep grinned. 'The gang leader – picked him up half an hour ago.'

'Whereabouts?' Geordie asked. 'Did he get far?'

'No, not very far,' said Sep. 'Found him in our back field.'

'Y' didn't shoot the bugger, did y'?'

'No,' said Sep laughing. 'I wouldn't do a thing like that.' He took a mug from Doreen and settled by the table.

'I'll tell y' what I think happened,' he said . . . 'I think the lad came into the field carryin' that bag o' money, the swag bag – and the bloody yowes thought it was feedin' time, so they came after 'im.' Sep stopped to take a drink, and maybe add just a touch of tension to the tale. 'Then the silly lad panics doesn't he. He thinks these creatures are comin' to attack 'im – so he starts t' run. Well of course the quicker he runs the quicker they follow . . . they'd be blarin' their heads off by now likely. Y' know what they're like at this time of year . . . absolutely ravenous, no grass . . . one sniff of anything that looks like a feed bag, and they just go crackers. They've knocked me down many a time!' He took another drink of tea.

'So anyway,' says Sep, 'he's runnin' like the wind, isn't he – lookin' back over his shoulder at these hungry mules gainin' on him all the time . . . and you'll never guess what happens . . .?' Geordie didn't answer . . . just looked at Sep, and waited. . . .

'Well, about a week ago,' Sep went on, 'we had a dead yow, and I says t' Willie, I says just drag her out o' sight and bury the bitch. Well, Willie buries her alright, but he doesn't hap 'er up does he? He figures there'll surely be a few more dead 'n's before we're finished, so he digs a good bit deeper – and leaves the muckle great hole open. . . .' They were both smiling now.

'I'm not sure that's legal anymore,' says Geordie.

Sep ignored him. 'Anyway along comes our little burglar friend – fleein' from about fifty mad yowes 'n' twins. . . . He's frightened half t' death, covered in shit, still clingin' onto his ill-gotten gains . . . not lookin' where he's goin' of course . . . and cowps straight into the pit, on top o' the dead yow – wham! I found 'im sittin' in there this mornin', about nine o'clock. The sheep were all standin' round the hole still blarin' at 'im. I think he broke a leg. He was nea bother. . . .'

Geordie took a sip from his mug. 'Sep,' he said thought-fully, 'you're definitely not feedin' those yowes o' yours plenty, y' know. . . .'

EPILOGUE

Five weeks after the Hindburn affair, Northumbria Police were called to check out a hired Ford Mondeo, apparently abandoned in the long-stay parking area at Newcastle Airport. According to the ticket stuck to the windscreen, the car had been there since early on Tuesday March 26th.

There were no useful prints to be found on the vehicle, inside or out . . . but a thorough inspection subsequently revealed tyre treads matching perfectly the mysterious wheel marks discovered in a grass field near Haugh House, the day after the robbery and murder.

Further enquiries led to a car rental company in Leeds, who readily provided the usual documented details given by the man who hired the car for one week on March 23rd . . . paying cash.

A statement given by Gloria Swanson had already mentioned her visitor on the night of the robbery. The man certainly drove a similar black Mondeo, but she couldn't recall the number, and gave only a vague description of the driver. She thought he might've been foreign. His phone call that night was eventually traced to a public call box in Glasgow. The Air UK desk at Newcastle Airport confirmed the same man had almost certainly boarded the early flight to Brussels on the 26th. He had a ticket purchased several days earlier in Paris, and gave his name on both transactions (car hire and flight) as Jacques Lapin.

The significance of this unlikely name finally registered

with Inspector Moffatt, when he listened again to the last two recorded messages received by Giles Pollock.

He immediately contacted Interpol . . . but with very meagre expectations. It seemed reasonable to assume 'the rabbit catcher' had long since gone to ground, and vanished into some obscure Euro-burrow.

FARMING PRESS BOOKS & VIDEOS

Other books by Henry Brewis also published by Farming Press are:

Country Dance   The story of a family farm and the triumphs (few) and disasters (many) it has witnessed over 60 years.

Chewing the Cud   The farming scene from a peasant's-eye view – the third cartoon collection.

Clarts and Calamities   The diary of a year in a peasant's life with its disasters (frequent) and triumphs (rare).

Don't Laugh Til He's Out of Sight   Stories, verses and illustrations revealing the hazards awaiting anyone venturing on life as a farmer.

Funnywayt'mekalivin'   The first collection of Henry Brewis's cartoons featuring Sep, the universal peasant.

Goodbye Clartiehole   Cartoons and written sketches covering modern agricultural 'developments' such as the IACs form as well as more traditional farm activities like sheepdog trials and harvest time.

Harvey and the Handy Lads   Henry's first book for children is an entertaining story aimed at 7- to 10-year-olds. Harvey the hedgehog dare not cross the road because so many animals have been squashed by the dangerous vehicles which zoom along it every day. Read the book and discover the brilliant solution to his problem.

Shepherd's Pie   The wit and wisdom of Henry Brewis captured on a double cassette of stories and poems, all with a country theme, read by Henry himself. Classic sketches as well as new material.

The Magic Peasant   The second cartoon collection showing Sep in his world of collie dogs, auctioneers, sheep and the long-suffering wife.

For more information or for a free illustrated catalogue of all our publications please contact:

Farming Press Books & Videos
Miller Freeman Professional Ltd
Wharfedale Road, Ipswich, Suffolk IP1 4LG, United Kingdom
Fax: (01473) 240501   Tel: (01473) 241122